THE CASINO

by

MARGARET BONHAM

with a new preface by

CARY BAZALGETTE

D1496972

PERSEPHONE BOOKS
LONDON

CONTENTS

PREFACE

One day in 1948, when I was six and my brother four, our mother disappeared. We were living at the time in Ware Cross, a sprawling '30s bungalow and smallholding on a stony hill-side above the Teign Valley in Devon. I have the tiniest memory, like a blurred snapshot, of a car jouncing away down the rough driveway between the unmown lawns and experimental vegetable beds, her hand flickering happily out of the window.

We did not see her again until 1950, when custody arrangements had been agreed with our father. Again, I have just a scrap of memory. We are in a railway station café and suddenly realise that the slim, blonde, smartly dressed woman sitting at a table across the room is actually our mother. We spring at her, expecting hugs and admiration, but she remains seated. As I try to clamber onto her I realise that we are tactlessly trying to re-enact some sloppy scene from books or films; sentimental displays of affection, especially in public, are not what this new relationship is going to be about. My own children, growing up in the huggy, kissy late twentieth century, will find this incomprehensible.

Of course we already knew then that she was a writer. When *The Casino* came out in 1948 I hoped that boasting about it would secure me the esteem of other children at school, but they had already decided that, since my mother had run away, I was obviously some sort of grotesque, an unlucky figure best avoided. I found a secluded wall to lean against in playtimes and tried to look nonchalant. I found out later from the stories that she, at least, appreciated me. 'One of them is about you', she had said. 'Read "The Professor's Daughter".'

These stories, then, stood in for my mother during my childhood and teenage years. I read and re-read them until I knew many of the sentences by heart. I relished the description of Britta's eyes in 'The Professor's Daughter': 'large, blank and brilliant, the colour of a sunless sea' and recognised them as mine; in the other stories I found more and more daughters: Vicky, Angela, Prue, Lin, Frankie, Annabel, and even the new baby in 'The Two Mrs Reeds'. Reassuringly for the Daughter Whose Mother Had Run Away, few of the children in these stories have two parents, and when they do ('The Train and the Gun') trouble looms. Family life in a conventional sense is non-existent here; it may be implied in 'The Professor's Daughter', 'The River' and in the Lucy and Louis stories ('The Miss' and 'The Two Mrs Reeds'), but in most cases the spouses are merely sketched in: the heart of each story is usually the relationship between one parent and a child.

It was much later that I developed a more ironic view: these stories had been written, after all, while my parents' marriage was breaking up. Did the stories stand in for her lost

relationships, as they did for me? I'll never know. But in any case it became increasingly more interesting to discover her life through the stories, to trace places and people re-made and re-worked for the public gaze.

So, many of the stories, whether they say so or not, are set in Devon where she and my father lived during and after World War II, and where my brother and I were born. My father was a conscientious objector and they had set up a sort of commune for pacifists in St Bridget, a large double-fronted eighteenth-century house on West Street in Ashburton, on the southern edge of Dartmoor. 'The River' is set in Ashburton and the river of the title is the Yeo, which you can still see from the little humped bridge off North Street, disappearing under the houses. 'Rolliver' documents the train that still runs up and down the Dart Valley between Ashburton and Totnes, whose engine in the 1940s was called Bulliver: all the anecdotes in this story (the cat, the pigeons, the goat, the inward-opening doors) are absolutely true. In each of the idyllic rural settings where she always managed to live, my mother in her role as Labour Party activist would inexorably track down whatever fragments of the industrial working class such places had to offer: this would usually turn out to be the railway workers, which in Ashburton resulted in my being able to clamber over Bulliver with the train driver and to have rides in the cab. Smaller hints reveal the Devon setting of other stories: the red cliffs and seaside location of 'The Train and the Gun' are on the main line west of Exeter where it runs close to the sea between Dawlish Warren and Teignmouth; the cliffs 'like slices of pink cake with green icing' in

'Vicky', together with the Georgian houses, set it in Sidmouth where my mother had gone for holidays as a child; the hospital setting of 'The Two Mrs Reeds' with its view of 'the distant harbour' is Torbay Hospital, where my brother and I were born; the legacy of the soldiers in 'Inigo' ('an indefinite number of white babies and three black ones' – so, implicitly, American soldiers) sets it in Ashburton immediately after the war, and even Milly's vulgar house in 'Miss King' is 'carved out of the desert moor': Ashburton again.

Other stories gave me glimpses of my mother's life before I was born. 'The Casino' is set in Wimereux on the French Channel coast near Calais, where she stayed for several months in the mid-'30s and arrived home in Wimbledon, she told me with relish, to scandalise her parents with her tiny new hat and a French accent. Scandalising her parents was one of my mother's major pastimes, and several of these stories show encounters between fusty outmoded attitudes and modern, open-minded lifestyles. Small-minded, prissy Miss Jenner is defeated by the freckled, untidy professor's wife in 'The Professor's Daughter'; the fluttering 'miss' subjects Lucy to the Lady Test in 'The Miss'. Other characters – Kitty in 'The Casino', Vicky, Emma in 'Miss King', and above all Lucy – represent the kind of daring, risk-taking, outspoken character that she liked to think her mother regarded with apprehension and disapproval.

But in fact my grandmother, born Edith Lorkin in Lavender Hill in 1886, was herself exactly that kind of character. In the 1900s she had a secretarial job in Bloomsbury and was writing amusing stories and sketches, reminiscent of Weedon

and Grossmith, with a fine ear for social comedy. Her marriage to Frank Bonham, a minor civil servant and Methodist lay preacher, nearly ten years older than her, put an end to such frivolous pursuits. She was expected to stop work, of course, and to concentrate on home-making in a nice new double-fronted house looking out onto South Park Gardens in Dudley Road, Wimbledon. If she needed to write at all, it should be essays on religious topics.

No doubt Edith saw Frank as quite a catch: he was dashingly good-looking with dark hair, blue eyes and a stylish moustache, a terrific athlete and widely respected in their set as a great intellect: in fact he simply had the Victorian male's fascination with unusual facts and remarkable phenomena, which he indefatigably listed and categorised. Edith was undoubtedly the brighter of the pair: more outgoing and more liberal in her views. She loved to show off and to tell risky stories; she scoured junk shops, not for Victorian tat but for industrial convex mirrors, laboratory glassware, catering crockery. By the time I knew Dudley Road in the late 1940s, it was painted white throughout in the style pioneered by Syrie Maugham in the '30s, with bare wooden floors and two aluminium reclining armchairs recovered from the saloon of a '30s airliner; she urged me to think about becoming an architect or a teacher, not a mere housewife. Edith was fundamentally frustrated: she nagged and dramatised while Frank became more preoccupied with his lists and with woodworking in the garden shed. He became an amateur astronomer and a Fellow of the Royal Astronomical Society, lugging his enormous brass telescope out into the back garden of a night, to study the moon.

Into this home their adored only daughter, Margaret, was born in October 1913 after a difficult labour (and after that they never had sex again, my mother said sourly). The photos show a beautiful, blonde, wavy-haired toddler with brilliant light eyes and admiring parents. Frank was too old to serve in the First World War but volunteered as a Special Constable and so was able to stay at home and see his daughter grow up. Maybe he is the model for the elderly father, William, in 'The River', who has such a placid and indulgent relationship with a daughter called Frankie.

For many years I mapped the stories in *The Casino* onto the real tensions between my mother and grandmother, constructing a drama out of the apparently unbridgeable gulf between bohemian daughter and suburban mother. There are recognisable fragments of my grandmother everywhere in the stories if you think you know where to look for them: Miss Ledwitch's lust for the blue vase; Miss Jenner's scything glance at the professor's wife's living-room (too full of books, too empty of furniture); Mrs Sedley's strictures on clean shoes and washbasins in 'The Horse'; the Miss's parsnip wine and embarrassing enthusiasm for foreigners.

Now, I see these traits as less important than the female power struggles that drive most of the narratives. Margaret's maternity wards, bridge parties and schools are more like competitive arenas than sororities. Her accounts of parenting always play out a culture clash, directly or indirectly. Mrs Sedley, and Mrs Keven in 'Annabel's Mother', are straightforwardly baffled by their children; William and Emmy in 'The River' are a living critique of conventional parental fussing;

the professor's wife knows she must humour Britta's fantasies rather than challenge them. Another arena for attitudinal struggle is – though this is never made explicit – between gay women and straight. Army Boots in 'The Miss' and Miss Howell in 'The Blue Vase' are caricature dykes, but Emma in 'Miss King' is beautiful and wise as well as tough and tweedy. The issue is not their sexuality, however, but their ability to be brutally frank about issues that the more bourgeois characters quail at.

Looking at these stories for evidence about what my mother thought herself to be, and by implication wanted me to be, I knew that the role model to go for was Lucy Furneaux in 'The Two Mrs Reeds'. Lucy is confident, knowledgeable, brisk, full of bravado and, rather more surprisingly, universally admired. She reads the *New Statesman* but she also wears candy-pink lipstick and has an exotic husband who brings her grey tulips. I knew she would look exactly like my mother, striding down West Street in her navy dungarees, climbing the cliffs rather than sitting on the beach. Lucy approves of everything my mother approved of: cats, Georgian houses, the Welsh, old cars, Vol de Nuit, Salvador Dali. If the stories were longer the list would no doubt be extended to include bridge, cricket, rugby, Bach, Beethoven and Shakespeare, and perhaps, too, the equally long list of things she disapproved of: opera, football, the Scots, jazz, musicals, knitting and anything Victorian.

In the '50s I loved these idiosyncratic lifestyle codes, which I uncritically adopted because they opened up a shared world with my mother. When I stayed with her, on the predetermined custody timetable, we could suddenly decide to drive to Wales

in the middle of the night, or sneak into ruined eighteenth century mansions, or go to Stratford to see the Oliviers in *Titus Andronicus*. It was only later that these attitudes began to seem arbitrary and petulant, more like teenage pretensions than solidly argued beliefs. So now, I still enjoy Lucy Furneaux in a nostalgic sense, but I also recognise her as one of the most aspirational, least credible women in *The Casino*. Nor am I very convinced by Harriet in 'Inigo', Celia in 'Rolliver' or Emmy in 'The River', who now seem just ciphers supporting a catalogue of my mother's attitudes. It is the women who change in the course of a story, who go through some kind of challenge and emerge at least unscathed, that I now find more interesting: Rhys in 'The Casino'; Mrs Keven; and even Mrs Miller in 'A Fine Place for the Cat'.

Most of the men in *The Casino* come in two types. There are the competent, amusing, kindly figures: Kendall in 'The Horse', Marston in 'Inigo', Dr Ferris in 'Annabel's Mother'. But there are also feebly pompous men who attempt to impose pointlessly authoritarian discipline: Henry in 'Rolliver', Thomas in 'The Two Mrs Reeds' and, by implication, the late Reverend Ignatius Jenner in 'The Professor's Daughter'. Anyone looking for male character sources in my mother's life has plenty to choose from. Her first husband was Walter Griffith, whom she married very young. I know little about Walter except that in the '30s he was a senior figure in the Peace Pledge Union (PPU); in fact I knew nothing of his existence until a school friend of mine had the temerity to read my mother's driving licence and found there the evidence that she had been married before she met my father:

for us as teenagers in the 1950s this was yet another terrible revelation about her moral turpitude, which I could hardly bear to contemplate, let alone ask about. But this first marriage was clearly a disaster. My grandmother liked to tell me how Margaret managed to get an annulment on the grounds of non-consummation, turning up to court in a gymslip, 'but' she added darkly, 'I found a used contraceptive in their wardrobe!' She may have meant that it was used by someone other than Walter, or that it was Walter's and therefore Margaret was lying; either way the message was that the non-virginal schoolgirl plaintiff had been lucky to get the annulment.

By this time Margaret had already met Deryck Bazalgette, a lanky, amusing young man of her own age, who had been born and brought up in Western Canada and then came back to England to attend public school at Lancing College, where he had been despised as a mere colonial but had developed strong Christian beliefs. He was working with a stockbroking firm in the City and enjoyed a busy social life as a member of the Wimbledon Cricket Club. At the start of the Munich crisis in 1938 he had joined the local branch of the Territorial Army, along with many of his friends. But after Chamberlain's betrayal of Czechoslovakia, his Christianity and his love for Margaret with her PPU affiliations led him to leave the Territorials, to the disgust and horror of his family and friends.

Margaret now owned an open-top Lagonda; he threw in the stockbroking job and they drove away to the Welsh borders, picking up bits of casual work here and there. Deryck remembers standing outside a youth hostel near Worcester on 3rd September 1939, listening to Chamberlain's broadcast coming from inside the house. They got married; he registered officially as a conscientious objector and was sent to work on the land. The Society of Friends helped them buy the big Ashburton house to use as a base for other 'conchies' and my father took on the task of finding agricultural jobs for a series of weird characters from London who seemed to be always bearded, beret-wearing or homosexual, and therefore objects of extreme suspicion to sceptical Devon farmers. There are thus elements of Deryck in Lucy's husband Louis, the most rounded male character in these stories. But Deryck was not French, despite his French surname. He was also not a farmer but a jobbing agricultural labourer earning £2 a week, who used an old pram to transport his tools, and cut such an unprepossessing figure that a passing motorist once tried to cadge some clothes coupons off him.

By 1942 Margaret was a mother and was becoming a writer. My father remembers her appearing at the smallholding where he was working, some time in 1943, with me on her hip, waving her first earnings: a cheque for $400 from an American magazine. In the exchange rates of the time this was just about what he earned in a whole year. Deryck had not been radicalised enough for him not to find it threatening to have a wife who could earn more than he did. Nevertheless my mother went on writing. Her emancipated female characters and confident, fluent style went on appearing in magazines such as *Modern Reading*, *English Story*, *Good Housekeeping* and *Harper's Bazaar*. An American air force base was set up near by: Margaret and her friend Jean got to

know the officers and would come back from dances to find my father waiting up for them, stern-faced and disapproving. In December 1944 my brother Charles was born but the marriage was already beginning to show signs of strain. My mother could write movingly about parents and children, but needed her own out of the way while she was doing it. I was packed off to a local school when I turned three: I know this because when my mother hauled me out of bed on VE night in June 1945 to watch the huge victory bonfire ('you'll remember this, my girl', she said, and I do) she put me into my new navy-blue school knickers to keep warm.

Amongst my parents' circle of conscientious objectors and Labour Party friends was Charles Kimber, who lived with his wife Ursula and three sons in a beautiful riverside house at Teigngrace, near Newton Abbot. He had been one of the founders of Federal Union in the 1930s, a movement for European political union. He was charming, intelligent, and despite having attended Eton and Balliol, politically left-wing. Both he and my mother were active in Labour politics in the lead-up to the 1945 General Election; he had just tried his hand at a novel and hugely admired her writing. They began to collaborate on writing a play, and of course they fell for each other. He recognised, but tolerated, the sentimentality and contradictions of her political beliefs. For all her assiduous cultivation of real-life working-class friends, there is a stiffness and condescension about the stories in *The Casino* that do not have a middle-class setting: 'The Train and the Gun' and 'A Fine Place for the Cat'; while the cockney Mrs Shellback in 'Inigo' is straight out of Ealing comedies.

Soon after the war ended St Bridget was sold and my father went into partnership with Terence Heelas, another 'conchie' friend, to develop a smallholding at Ware Cross, the hilltop house near Kingsteignton. We all moved in with Terence and his wife Mary in 1947. But Charles Kimber and my mother were determined to be together: 'we want each other!' he wrote to my father, with passionate underlining. My mother was with us at Ware Cross for a while – I can just remember seeing her and my father fighting on the stairs – but then came the day in 1948 when she went away to live with Kimber on the Thames, in a converted lifeboat where he was living while reading for a social anthropology diploma at Oxford. Mary Heelas remembers my brother and me as the unhappiest children she had ever seen. If we have grown up relatively sane, it is down to her loving commonsense, and perhaps also to the vast ramshackle playground of Ware Cross with its water tower, pigsties, greenhouses, and nearby woods.

But there was also, when we finally became aware of it, the increasingly fascinating world of our mother's new life. Three years after *The Casino* came her novel, *The House across the River* (not a success: the short story was her forte) and Charles Kimber inherited his father's baronetcy. My mother became a titled lady living in Judges, a seventeenth-century farmhouse in Oxfordshire, which she startlingly redecorated in the austere taste well documented in *The Casino*. They had a cook, a gardener and, when two more children came along, a nanny; there were two cars, soft toilet paper and Martinis before dinner. Our holidays (a week at Christmas and Easter, three in the summer) seemed an exotic contrast to our humdrum

existence in a tied cottage in Surrey where my father, now remarried, had become head gardener on the Earl of Drogheda's estate. Inbetween times she and I wrote reams of letters to each other. I was determined to become a writer like her. I wrote 'novels' which she typed and even sent to her agent, Dorothy Daly at Curtis Brown. I still have a letter of stylistic advice my mother sent me when I was about thirteen: don't repeat words; steer clear of exclamation marks; when in doubt about a comma, leave it out; don't forget the useful semi-colon; stick to 'said' rather than horrid words like 'chortled' or 'ejaculated'.

Margaret's income from writing was increasing, but now formed a relatively small proportion of the family finances. She became obsessed with her earning power as a writer, and desperate to break into the big time. Through the '50s and '60s her style lost its freshness and her plots became schematic romances and crime stories. By 1960 her marriage to Kimber had collapsed, and what seemed to me an idyll had ended. Geese wandered into the house and made a mess on the turquoise dining-room carpet; cats shredded the white silk armchairs; the children threw the Georgian silver down the well; the drinks weren't just before dinner. Rummaging about as usual in other people's wardrobes, my grandmother discovered the empties and estimated my mother's intake as eight bottles of gin a week: a remarkable total considering that she continued to drive everywhere (she would rather drive than walk fifty yards to the letterbox, and in later years would 'walk' her dog Daisy by shoving her out of the car to run along behind).

The crisis came in 1963 when her twelve-year-old daughter Rhys found her haemorrhaging from severe liver damage. She survived, but Judges was sold, she and Kimber divorced, and eventually she moved back to Devon, living first in a caravan and then in Lower Cottshayne, an ancient thatched cottage near the village of Colyton. Her parents, still wearily bailing her out, finally sold their house in Dudley Road and came to live nearby in Sidmouth. My mother began to settle to an apparently contented life alone: gardening, planting a wood of rare trees, keeping geese, a dog and a cat, chatting with farmers in the pub, continuing to write and to plan that elusive best-seller. But in 1972 came the bitterest blow of her life: her son Justin was killed in a car crash just days after his nineteenth birthday. She seemed to cope, but she never wrote again.

She stayed on in Devon: her parents died; my husband and I brought our children to visit each Easter but after a few disastrous attempts to stay at Cottshayne agreed that we would rather stay in nearby farms than endure her irritation at our invasion of her routines. She moved eventually to a 1920s semi-detached house in Colyton but still had an enormous garden and amusing friends. Having been an enthusiastic smoker all her life it came as no great surprise when she was diagnosed with advanced lung cancer in 1991. 'I'm glad,' she said to me on the phone, 'I don't want to be old.' She refused treatment and in November, unable to bear the suffocating pressure of the growing tumour, she took an overdose and died in her sleep.

At her funeral, her sixteen-year-old granddaughter Phoebe read the last two sections of 'The Professor's Daughter'. We felt it was important to remember, not only her achievement as a writer, but also the poignancy of that 'absent care'. Margaret's two surviving husbands, both now in their nineties, remember her with wistful affection; she was certainly impossible to live with, but she is also impossible to forget.

Cary Bazalgette
London, 2003

THE CASINO

THE CASINO

Badgered by the English, Mademoiselle at last said she would go and ask Giselle's father. She took off her apron, and in the black dress with the lilac frill, pinned at the neck by a brooch with a picture of Napoleon's tomb, she went down the street towards the sea and turned through the gate of the white house Sainte Claire. Here she was received in the salon; here M. Chabouillard stood majestic and pale as mutton-fat in his rococo setting, touching the waxed ends of his moustache with an alabaster finger and thumb. Mademoiselle found the salon intimidating. The chairs were heavily beaded, and Mme Chabouillard, heavily beaded too, sat on one of them twisting her rings in their grooves. No Napoleon's tomb for her; a diamond brooch as big as a saucer lay so flat on her bosom she could have put a cup on it. In her cotton dress, with her knees apart, she sat uneasily and looked from the carpet to her husband, and sideways at the visitor, and back to the carpet again.

Mademoiselle took time to come to the point, and the longer she took the more her throat seemed likely to dry up on the word Casino. Breathing deeply, she plunged into one of M. Chabouillard's pauses, which were becoming interrogatory

and would soon be less pause than silence. 'The English young ladies wish me to ask you if you would permit Giselle . . .' Round and round went Madame's rings; M. Chabouillard grew perceptibly larger. He enunciated with care, putting up a hand as if to catch and subdue his active moustaches. 'Who would then accompany them?'

'They desire to go alone.' Mademoiselle looked down at her slippers, admired their looped bows. Now that it was out she felt ready for battle; on this beaded bird she would sit till it stamped her flesh with a pattern, before she would give in to the Chabouillards. She spoke of English emancipation and told them how reliable were her pupils, how discreet and sensible. 'Of very good family,' she said, attacking with trumps. But M. Chabouillard had met the English; she saw in his eye the questions she asked herself, the doubts whether young ladies of good family, even in England, were quite so . . . could be so very . . .

'To be allowed at the tables,' said Mademoiselle quickly, 'one must be twenty-one. It would be merely an affair of the café for an apéritif, perhaps a little dancing among themselves, a promise to be home by ten — After all, it is not Monte Carlo, this place.'

'Evidemment,' said M. Chabouillard. She looked up from her slippers and met his jellied stare.

Meanwhile the English waited, sprawled on the steps that led from the house down to the sandy garden where shells cracked under one's feet. Rhys and Valentine wore shorts and Kitty a bathing-suit in two very small pieces. The Channel lay

milky-blue across the end of the street. On the foolish houses, on their pink turrets and curled balconies, fell a light like a sword.

'I wish she would hurry,' said Rhys, conscientiously in French.

'I wish Giselle didn't have to come,' said Valentine in English.

Rhys said silently, I wish we didn't have to go at all. Anything might happen at a Casino.

'She thinks it looks better,' said Kitty, 'in case we get raped.'

'But Giselle is much more likely —'

'Then, you see, she has it both ways, she could tell the Chabouillards it was Giselle's own fault, provided with three chaperoning foreigners. Foreigners, but after all, *three* —'

'I wouldn't stop it. I feel sure it would do her good.'

'We can't go if it rains,' said Rhys despairingly, making a feeble effort to get away from rape. Kitty looked at her with contempt, and then up at the sky, and did not even answer.

'Here she comes,' said Valentine.

Mademoiselle in her crackling slippers opened the iron gate. Her behind stuck out, faintly patterned with a bird. Across the garden, between her and the English, a gulf stretched as wide as the Channel, between their limbs displayed and her lilac frills and Napoleon's tomb. 'Eight o'clock. He has given his permission.' She smiled complacently.

'How wonderful,' said Rhys. A little too loudly, a shade too soon; but Kitty and Valentine shouted, leaped, and did not notice.

Rhys ironed her dark-red frock in the kitchen, for once alone. Cold struck from the stone floor up her bare legs, down towards it plunged her anxious stomach. Anything might happen at a Casino. After dark, abroad, alone. Gambling, and strange foreigners. In case we get raped. Drink. Mademoiselle clapped out of the scullery with a pile of mussels on a dish. 'Enfin, vous êtes contente?'

'Je suis bien heureuse.'

Kitty and Valentine were in the attic bedroom. Valentine with the canvas propped on a chair was painting the window and the view of turrets and sea. Kitty was applying blue oil paint to her eyelids. In the room's disorder two long dresses were laid reverently, one on the double brass bed, one on the single iron one; from the table, the chest, the chairs and the washstand a confusion of clothes and whatnots dripped and overflowed on the bare wood floor. 'Suppose someone asked me to dance,' Kitty was saying, '"Avec plaisir, monsieur" would probably be best. Or just getting up.'

'Suppose someone did, he might be English.'

'If he's English I shall pretend to be French. If he's French I shall be a Swede, I think.'

Valentine painted Kitty's red bathing-suit, which hung damp on the window-sill; in the picture it was not red but greenish-grey. Kitty's head, with bluish eyelids and a scarf round the hair, was thrust between the brush and the canvas. 'Sans blague,' she said, 'how is this?'

'I dare say it won't look *quite* so tarty in electric light.'

Mademoiselle, in black from head to foot, threw up her hands at Kitty's black frock, at Valentine's grey one too discreetly striped with gold. 'O ciel,' she said, 'time to wear black and grey when troubles come, and come they will,' she assured them. 'Every day,' said Kitty in English, 'I think the French are more dotty.' Waiting for the soup, she stood with one elbow on the Indian shawl that draped the piano, full of power from the touch of black net on her ankles, from her blue eyelids and the light curl set to fall over one eye. Valentine stared at Mademoiselle; she saw her in a frame black and pale beside the horsehair sofa, with a plucked chicken on a dish. The bird's flesh and Mademoiselle's would be the same colour, greenish like clay. Nature Morte. Rhys in the corner fidgeted over the dictionary; with her dark-red dress, her rough dark hair set by Kitty in a roll on top of her head, she had a Persian air; she was asking herself what she would do if a man accosted them on the way to the Casino. Out loud she said, 'I wish it were eight o'clock.' Marie brought in the soup.

One of Rhys's moments of pure horror engulfed her. Macaroni letters floated in the bouillon spelling fear in her plate; and there she sat, abroad, alone, in a dark dining-room, with Kitty and Valentine not familiar in school uniform but dressed up like loose women to visit a gaming-house; no past in this dwelling but the war twenty years into history, no future but the war yet untold and yet unloosed, already rehearsing in Spain. On the thread of the horrid present, Rhys swung between.

'Mademoiselle Rhys, you do not eat.'

'I'm too excited.'

In the dusk, Giselle waited outside the iron gates. Her frock was pink and stuck out like a cake-frill, she undulated and giggled. In a line of four they went down the street towards the sea, past Sainte Claire where Giselle waved and Valentine looked sideways seeing M. Chabouillard's face a round, whiskered, disapproving moon at the window. Between Kitty's steel confidence and Valentine's detachment, Rhys walked with her eyes on the heaving Channel, thinking of ruin. Across her, Kitty and Valentine (those nice girls, Rhys's parents said; if they could see them now) flung remarks in Cockney, for Giselle had some English, but Cockney defeated her. The Casino stood naked on a low cliff, beyond the promenade; like a great hollow tank, faintly lit, it was jettisoned between the sea and the sky. On the sweep of gravel one car was abandoned; beyond it, a gun emplacement added the future to Rhys's dismal present. The swing doors opened like a mouth, breathing warm air.

The foyer was deserted, denying Kitty an entrance which, even impeded by three female companions, might in her hopes have caused a stir; there was no one to whisper, no one to stare, and indeed (thought Kitty with rising annoyance at the misguided hour) for all the audience she had she might have been dressed as Harpo Marx without attracting a second glance. Behind the little desk a vast Madame with purple hair took their piles of francs, handed them pink tickets with a flourish sketching irony. And now there was nothing to do but wait, but sit in a row of three on a red plush seat, with Kitty on a gilt chair refusing a row of four; there was nothing to do but wait, and nothing to say.

Giselle was in the Casino, without Papa; her reaction was simple pleasure.

Valentine was shaping the evening in acceptance. Like Giselle, she was content to receive but in order to create. No line or tone of the Madame at the desk escaped her stare; her mind swallowed into memory the texture of pink décolletage, the black satin bosom, the magenta ridged hair. Portrait: the Casino. Awareness separated Valentine like glass. She looked from the Madame to Giselle, discovering untold why the French painted their mouths bow-shaped, the English oblong. From the French side she saw Kitty and Rhys across the gulf.

Rhys was suspended like one who, sitting in the dentist's chair, suffers discomfort but waits for pain. Catastrophe was surely yet to come; she sat disbelievingly among the spotty mirrors and gilded cupids, with a fixed willing air. Memory heaved up a scene of prostitutes in a film, waiting on a plush seat along a wall. Rhys turned an appalled gaze on Kitty's eyelids.

Kitty's reactions were as simple as Giselle's. She was possessed by threefold fury, because they were too early, and no one would talk, and she of all people was embarrassed. She smiled with parted lips sideways at the mirrors.

Before nine o'clock a little boy ran across the chessboard floor, pulling tight over his belly the lowest of twenty buttons. Madame shook out pink powder in a cloud, brushed purple hairs and this and that from her shoulders. 'On arrive,' said Giselle, and painted a cerise bow, for Papa was, after all, well out of the way. The doors swung open on the dark, and people began to come in; even the lights went up. In Kitty,

relief fought with shamed anger towards Rhys and Valentine and Giselle, who gaped at the entrance like brats at a party; except obliquely she would not look at the arrivals. 'Keety,' said Giselle, leaning over, past blushing for, 'Keety, a so 'andsome man comes.' But Kitty, seeing him in the mirror, said with a touch of venom, 'Only dagoes have side-whiskers.' 'Comprends pas,' Giselle said to Valentine, who, grinning, put up her hands and drew a line from temples to jaw. 'Elle dit que c'est une mode pour les étrangers.' Giselle was baffled: 'Mais c'est un français, celui-là.' 'Oh, shut up, for God's sake,' said Kitty, burning under the dago's amused glance. She must talk, but there was nothing to say; she must appear worldly, but the others weighed her down. Now the foyer was quite full of people, but few lingered; they streamed under the arch, through the swing doors into the gaming-room, to play roulette. Courage rose in Kitty suddenly, taking her breath. She got up and walked away towards the arch. Valentine called after her, 'Where are you going?' but she would not look back. She was six months older than the others, and would soon be eighteen. In a little black quilted handbag she had eleven francs. Her knees shook.

Nothing was lost on the others; Kitty felt their six eyes, amused, appalled and curious, burning into her back. Triumph would have protected it, but the attendant under the arch barred her way. 'Mademoiselle est trop jeune; mademoiselle n'a pas le droit —' Kitty, whose ambition was the stage, found in pure panic the right deceiving gestures; the spotlight of necessity fell on her and she acted because she must. Pleased instead of defeated she returned, and answered 'Wouldn't he

let you in?' with 'He said you were all too young, and I didn't want to go by myself.' Rhys and Giselle were expressionless, perhaps awed; only Valentine looked with malice towards the attendant, said with malice, 'I'll go and ask him again.' Kitty turned the challenge down. Falsely uncaring, she said to Rhys and Giselle, 'Let's find the café and get something to drink.'

The word Drink hit Rhys in the wind. The night was full of evil words, Paint, Gambling, Men, and now Liquor. As lightly as Kitty, almost with pleasure and anticipation, she said, 'What can we have?' But Kitty made no reply. Even her walk, as they followed her, seemed to Rhys faintly indecent.

The restaurant was half-full, stuck with pink paper roses in white and gilt trellis. At the far end a damp, pink band played, the floor was cleared for dancing, the tables crowded round the walls. Kitty looked sulky, and ordered coffee without asking if anyone wanted something else, and at this Rhys was very much relieved, for her anxious fears had drawn a table covered with bottles of brandy, the bill paid by a leering stranger and Kitty the receipt. In her dark-red dress that gave her no pleasure she sat breathing carefully with her back to the wall. Valentine watched the dancers to find a face, a colour, a line of skirt or limbs, contented to observe. Giselle just watched them. Kitty looked for someone to take her away from this dreary group, someone to ask her to dance, the ultimate success. Nobody spoke.

After a long silence, Valentine said without embarrassment, 'I should quite like to dance.'

'Alone?' said Kitty savagely.

'I thought with you or Rhys.'

Kitty went pale with rage. Rhys said uneasily, 'I don't think —' shifting on the gilt chair, stared at by Giselle.

'Well, all right,' said Valentine, 'I don't mind. Watching people is just as good, but there *are* two women dancing together over there.'

Kitty turned a stony face. Her experience encompassed no more than a sense that to dance with one's own sex was the final degradation, the advertisement of failure to find a partner of the opposite. Hope and confidence had soured in her, and she wanted now to go home. The coffee was tepid; on the other tables glasses reflected the lights, translated them in rose and green and magenta. No one had spoken to her, asked her to dance, even smiled or looked in admiration; she was branded Adolescent with the others and could not get away. Under the dusty roses a clock said twenty to ten. M. Chabouillard was a cold breath on Giselle; Kitty and Rhys with separate impatience watched the minute hand drag to the quarter. Pride forced on both of them an air of reluctance when the moment came to go.

Across the chessboard floor of the hall Kitty almost ran, stung with shame to be leaving before ten like schoolgirls on a late pass. 'Bonne nuit, mes enfants,' said the great Madame at the desk. The last indignity; Kitty felt the prick of tears. Outside, the cold gravel in the dark turned and tripped her heels, and people climbed out of cars and passed her towards diversion just beginning.

Rhys should have been happy in the escape from danger, in the knowledge that it was over and of all the things that

might have happened not one had in fact occurred. But no indeed; now in the cold dark she clamped her teeth together to stop them from chattering and walked in returning fear of war and foreigners and being abroad. Giselle hurried to placate Papa; Valentine, smiling, looked back from the empty promenade to the Casino's lights. 'It was lovely,' she said.

Kitty ran away along the sea front, headlong towards home, knowing yet that it was not home and knowing in despair the alien winter to come. The flat sea and the thin moon were like a painted backcloth, the stage and theatre empty; with the hem of her frock torn by her heels that tapped so mournfully on the cold stone, Kitty wept as she ran.

Valentine put out a hand to Rhys who would have followed her. Rhys stared anxiously after Kitty up the promenade, which at night was sinister, deserted and dimly lit, and back to Giselle who had stopped under a lamp and was wiping off her lipstick with a red chiffon handkerchief. Emotion on arrival was a new storm looming; in real desperation Rhys clasped her hands and stood waiting.

Valentine, among all these panics and apprehensions, watched Giselle in a circle of light against the dark sea and the shore, and had only one pleasurable fear, which was that she would not be able to paint from memory the colour of Giselle's pink frock in the greenish lamplight.

VICKY

From the shore side a skin of light lay on each pool, the reflection of the sky; but with one's back to the sea the water in each hollow, fringed with brown weed, was clear as gin. Rose-coloured crabs, no bigger than a finger-nail, scuttled in the one Vicky crouched over, and dark-blue mussel shells lay like ships in the drowned sand. Moving carefully so that the shadow of her head should not break the light on the water she slid her hand into a cleft and touched an anemone; its crimson fingers clung instantly and delicately to hers, and then with an almost human change of temper pushed them aside. Tiny fish like sticks exploded away under the weeds. Vicky took her arm out of the pool. She sat back on her heels and wondered vaguely about the time; they had said half an hour. Sliding over the seaweed she began to make her way back to the promenade, stopping to linger over other pools and jab at the limpets to see them fasten against the rock. On the sands, scarred with anonymous and purposeful footprints, she did not run but went on walking with longer strides. She wore grey flannel shorts like a little boy's, and her hair was tied out of the way with a stringy ribbon. A length

of seaweed flapped and curled behind her, swung from one hand.

On a painted iron seat facing the sea the three aunts waited. Behind them the row of flat Georgian houses, their gardens gritty with sand, were closed and withdrawn from the sun, the striped blinds lowered. At either end the cliffs, like slices of pink cake with green icing, shut out the view and enclosed the bay.

'Oh, there you are, Vicky,' said Aunt Agnes.

'Are you wet?' said Aunt Marianne.

'Did you have a lovely game in the pools, dear?' said Aunt Violet.

Answering Aunt Marianne, Vicky examined the seat of her shorts and said 'No.' She stood in front of the three of them with her thin legs apart, her feet in damp sandals and the trail of seaweed picking up dust and sand from the pavement. They sat there quietly with their faces towards the sea, waiting for the eldest to make a move. This was Aunt Agnes. Her brown straw hat with the bird on top bowed, quivered with indecision, then flew into the air; Aunt Agnes, beneath it, had got briskly to her feet. Then Violet and Marianne followed. In a line of four they began to walk along the front, with Vicky nearest the sea flapping the seaweed and kicking at pebbles with her sandals.

Suddenly towards them came a car that made them stare, old almost as a car could be, spidery, but clean and glittering with brass. Out of an earlier age it swayed and tottered along the promenade, among the smooth curved saloons of the present; two young men, with the proud yet sheepish air of

those whose aim it is to be the centre of attention, sat high on the buttoned seats. 'Oh look, Violet – Marianne,' cried Aunt Agnes, 'an old car! Don't you remember? It's like George's.' They stood still, turned away from the sea, watching it pass like children at a circus.

'Oh, how it takes one back,' said Aunt Violet. 'Don't you remember, Agnes, how we used to sit all tied up in veils? And the things that went wrong, and the *dust*. Look, Vicky, at the old car, do you see it, dear? Your father had one just like that, when he was twenty-one.'

'Gosh,' said Vicky, 'the brake's on the outside. Aunt Violet, look at the brake. It's *outside*.'

'Is it?' said Aunt Violet. 'I remember George talking about the brake,' she said. She looked at Vicky with fawn's eyes, back in her Edwardian youth. The spidery car danced and winked itself out of sight, along the front.

'There, it's gone,' said Aunt Agnes. 'Come, don't stand still, Vicky; we've no time. Mrs Casey is coming at a quarter to one, and you have to change.'

'Oh gosh, must I? What into? Can't I —'

'No,' said Aunt Agnes, 'you cannot. We think those shorts are not quite nice even on the beach, but we must move with the times, and if the other children wear them we cannot let you be conspicuous. But for lunch with visitors, Vicky, we prefer you to be properly dressed, and I hope you will try to make a good impression on Mrs Casey, because she is an old friend of our family. She has not seen you for ten years; you were not quite two when she knew you last, at the – before you came to live with us.'

'Was I? Do you mean I've got to wear a frock?'

'Certainly a frock, dear. The blue one.'

'The BLUE one, oh gosh, Aunt Agnes —'

'The blue one, dear, and your new stockings.'

'STOCKINGS! Oh gosh, can't I just —'

'And your black slippers; don't argue, dear. We think that would be best, don't we, Violet?'

'Charming, Agnes,' said Violet, still in 1905, driving in a high-buttoned car with a young man called Alex; from behind the purple veil her deer's eyes looked at him, seeing him stiff and handsome in a high white collar. 'Will you marry me?' he had said suddenly, the car swayed to a standstill and the dusty light fell warm on their cheeks and hands, and she had cried out 'No. No, no,' she said, 'you don't understand – it's impossible. My mother —' Aunt Violet began to walk more quickly; she was three paces ahead of the others. When they reached the gate of their house she unlatched it and went up the path first, standing irresolutely by the red geraniums while they followed. The house was flat and still in the sun, bleached white as salt, the oblong windows dark. In front of it the sandy garden flowered round a lawn, the path was gritty with broken shells. There was a pile of seaweed beside the front door, that Vicky brought back with her from days on the beach; it was not allowed in the house, and the crust on it was dried by the sun. Aunt Marianne said it would rot and be good for the garden. 'Like horse-dung?' asked Vicky. Aunt Marianne said yes, and Aunt Agnes added that that was not a pretty word to use. Vicky dropped today's piece of seaweed on top of the pile. The sunblinds, striped in green and white and

red, were drawn down over the windows, and the shadows they cast were flecked with light from the sea. Aunt Agnes first, and then the other two and then Vicky, they went indoors.

All that could be done to turn a Georgian house into an Edwardian one, the aunts had spent much time over. The beautiful plain fireplaces of pearl-coloured marble they could not alter, but little fretwork shelves over the mantelpieces held china vases and silver frames and pigs with ferns growing out of their backs. The light filtered through lace curtains on to bamboo tables, stools inlaid with mother-of-pearl, pale chintz on the settees and chairs. Faint gilded water-colours were crowded on the satin-striped walls. The rooms were cool and smelt very slightly of camphor.

Vicky changed into the blue frock in her bedroom, unwillingly – it was the sort of frock she hated. The right people for smocked blue velvet were the people with curls and fat arms. Sand poured out of her shoes when she took them off, sitting on the floor, and piled itself on the pink carpet. She put on stockings and the black slippers, and deferring as long as possible the moment when she must go down to the drawing-room she looked at herself lingeringly and dispassionately in the glass while she brushed her hair. But this was a mistake; awareness of the something wrong in her appearance made her incapable now of moving naturally – her elbows stuck out, her frock became too long, her skin felt tight and her feet enormous. At the bottom of the stairs there were sounds, a counterpoint of voices from behind the closed door, that told her the visitors had come. Short of annoying Aunt Agnes, she could not put it off any longer. She turned the white china

handle under the white china fingerplate with painted roses, and went inside.

The blue frock was Vicky's sacrifice to Mrs Casey, and no more than that and a trained politeness could be expected of her; but Mrs Casey had brought her granddaughter with her. Like a suspicious kitten, Vicky stiffened. The grandchild was about thirteen; she had a rubber doll's face, with no bones in it, and round glasses, but she wore a plain navy frock with a red belt. Freckles and bones were better than glasses and a face like a bun, but Vicky eyed the navy frock with anguish. Eyeing it, she felt herself smocked from head to foot.

As for Mrs Casey, she was one of those people whose features, when one looks away from them, might never have existed. No one could have painted a portrait of her; there was simply nothing there to draw. As though she realised this, and wanted to make her personality heard or distract attention from her face, she was dressed with a rich magnificence and hung with beads. Beside her the aunts were thin Edwardian shadows, their wreck of beauty colourless; there was nothing Edwardian about Mrs Casey.

Vicky stood in front of her, shook hands and was taken in from head to foot. She fixed her eyes on Mrs Casey's bosom, which bore a ruby brooch like a soup plate. Tell Vicky, said Aunt Agnes's mind, she must look at people when she is introduced. I wonder if that brooch is real. Either way it's ostentatious. 'So this is poor little Vicky,' said Mrs Casey. 'How are you, dear? She has poor George's eyes.' Poor? Vicky looked enquiringly at the rubies.

'And Vicky,' said Aunt Agnes a shade quickly, 'this is Mrs Casey's daughter's little girl, Henrietta. She has very kindly brought her along to have a nice game with you.'

Vicky's lip curled back over her teeth and she and Henrietta shook hands with mutual dislike. 'Well,' said Mrs Casey (whose conversation went with her face and not her clothes), 'how sweet to see them together. They're almost the same age, aren't they? Last time I saw you, Vicky, you were in a pram. It always amazes me how quickly children grow up – it *is* amazing, isn't it?'

'Yes, it is,' said Vicky politely to the brooch, supposing this remark to be addressed to her.

They went in to lunch.

Vicky and Henrietta sat side by side in hostile silence. Vicky worked her sandy toes around inside her stockings till the skin was sore; Aunt Violet kept looking at her and Henrietta and then at Mrs Casey with hopeful smiles, as if to say 'How charming, aren't they dears?' Aunt Agnes talked to Mrs Casey about relations, and Aunt Marianne folded herself in one of her detached ironical silences; every now and then she came out of it to say 'No, Agnes, it was in '21, I think,' or 'Lucy was Alan's cousin, not his niece, surely.' The dining-room was like a dark oil-painting, all the light in it was held by the glass and silver and the damask cloth that gleamed like thawing snow. 'You remember Mrs Canning at Launceston —' said Aunt Agnes. In despair Vicky turned to Henrietta, who ate things self-consciously with a fork. 'Do you like dogs?' she said hoarsely.

'No,' said Henrietta.

'I do.'

'I don't,' said Henrietta. 'They're so rough.'

Vicky looked at her sideways, appalled. After a silence she said, 'Well, cats aren't.'

'Cats aren't what?'

'Rough.'

'Well, some are. Ours was.'

'Was it? I don't like them much.'

'Well, nor do I.'

Vicky shifted about on the chair and went on eating, remembering not to let her table-napkin slide to the floor and torn between hunger and her orders not to finish before the visitors were through.

'. . . in '24, when poor George married,' said Mrs Casey. That word again, thought Vicky. She wondered if she was poor because she was an orphan, and her father because he was dead. But he had been forty when he married and forty-five when he died; quite old. 'Of course,' said Mrs Casey, 'that was before —' Vicky saw Aunt Agnes look at her in an odd way. 'Yes, of course,' said Aunt Agnes; 'before Vicky was born.' 'Yes – yes, before Vicky was born,' said Mrs Casey. 'And James Radcliff – have you heard of him since then? He went to India, didn't he?' Vicky looked at Aunt Agnes; Aunt Agnes was faintly pink. She said, 'I believe he did, but I haven't heard of him for years.'

As she spoke she saw herself bare-shouldered in a white dress, with roses on the hem. It was 1901: she was twenty. She was crying, and James stood beside her, shut off from the rest by palms in gilded baskets. She said, 'I've told you, I can't

marry. I can never marry. I've told you why none of us can.'
'But you love me,' said James. 'That doesn't matter, what
you told me. We needn't – it doesn't make any difference.'
'No,' she cried, 'no, don't ask me.' And she ran, with her white
skirt catching in her white satin heels, to her brother George.
'We must put up with it,' said George in a flat voice. 'We can't
do anything about it. None of us can marry. We must just go
without.' He was only seventeen. And then twenty-three years
later, at George's wedding, she had seen James again. She
wore black silk gloves, and they drank champagne. The awful
sense of disaster she could remember clearly even now. 'It all
seems so long ago,' Aunt Marianne said placidly to Mrs Casey,
who cried, 'Oh no – no, not to me, I can see it as if it were
yesterday; the ball at the Castle, and what Lady Hand wore,
and their son – what was it? – Nicholas.'

Nicholas. Aunt Marianne remembered Nicholas saying,
half-seriously, 'I shall challenge Richard to a duel'; and she
had said, 'Oh, do be sensible – I am not going to marry
either of you. I am going to be a spinster with six cats.' Aunt
Marianne put down her fork and smiled; she had no cat at
all. 'How sad it is,' said Mrs Casey, helping herself brightly
to a glass of water. This time all the aunts gave her that odd
look.

'Things are so different now,' said Aunt Agnes. 'Cars
everywhere, and broadcasting and air travel. Are you settled
at Longhurst?' She drew Mrs Casey into the present, but it
was as uninteresting to Vicky as the past, except that there was
no mystery about it. She made another effort, and said to
Henrietta, 'Where do you go to school?'

'I don't,' said Henrietta complacently. 'I've got a governess.'

'Have you? How awful.'

'It isn't awful.'

'We play hockey and netball at my school. We —'

'I don't like games. We go for walks in the country and look for birds.'

'Good Lord.'

'Don't you like birds?'

'Hate them.'

There was another long silence. Vicky finished her pudding as soon as Henrietta's plate was empty, and Aunt Agnes got up and led the way back to the drawing-room. Henrietta tripped behind her jangling grandmother, and Vicky, bored, wishing she were on the beach finding things in pools, brought up the rear. Aunt Agnes sat in a pale-rose armchair and beckoned her over with one finger. 'Vicky, dear, would you and Henrietta like to go and play in the garden? I expect we shall go on talking about people you've never heard of, really you might as well be in the fresh air. Don't get too hot.'

'No, Aunt Agnes,' said Vicky. That she should get too hot playing with Henrietta seemed to her indeed unlikely. 'Come on,' she muttered; she pushed Henrietta through the hall and out into the blanched sunlight. The sea was stretched flat and glittering from the horizon, too bright to be more than faintly blue. Henrietta screwed up her eyes and adjusted her glasses. Vicky sighed. 'That's my pile of seaweed,' she said. 'I bring a piece back every day. It makes horse-dung for the garden.'

'You can't make horse-dung out of seaweed,' said Henrietta in a superior way.

'How do you know? You don't live by the seaside. Do you want to go on the beach?'

Henrietta looked vaguely at the garden, the shells and pebbles ground into the whitish path, the grass thin with sand, the coarse bright thickly-growing flowers. 'Your aunt told you here,' she said, 'but I shouldn't think they'd mind if we just went across the road. If it wouldn't spoil your frock,' she added with a touch of malice.

'Oh, it's an old one,' said Vicky instantly. 'It did come from Liberty's, in London, you know. I've had it ages now, I'm just wearing it out when it doesn't matter. But you ought to be careful of yours. Did your governess make it?' She was pleased to see that Henrietta was annoyed. Voices came drowsily through the open shaded window; Vicky heard Mrs Casey say, in a low tone, 'But how dreadful, but what a shock for you: weren't you horrified when he said he meant to marry? And Celia was quite young, wasn't she? Do you think she knew?' 'We have no idea,' said Aunt Agnes. 'We scarcely met her. As you know, she died soon after George . . .'

'You're eavesdropping,' said Henrietta, shocked.

'Oh, shut up and come on,' muttered Vicky. 'So were you.' They went out of the white gate and across the road and a strip of grass to the shore. Through her black slippers the shingle pressed knobs into Vicky's feet, even the warmth of it came through the thin soles. She put a stone on top of the breakwater, lifted up her frock to sit down and began throwing at it, and Henrietta, after a minute, joined in; she threw from the shoulder, very wide, in a helpless ladylike way, and Vicky looked at her with scorn. 'You do it all wrong,' she said. 'You throw like a girl.'

'I *am* a girl,' said Henrietta coldly, abandoning the game. Vicky knocked the stone off, set up another and went on playing. She wondered how long Mrs Casey would stay; as soon as they left she could put on her shorts again and go down to the rocks. But time seemed to be endless. She and Henrietta stayed sitting on the shingle. Once Henrietta said, 'I don't think I ought to be out here without a hat. I had sunstroke last summer.' 'Did you? So did I,' said Vicky immediately. 'I had my big toenails off, too.' Henrietta's glasses flashed a temporary interest; she asked, 'What for?' Fishing for her suspenders and peeling off her stocking, Vicky held out a sandy foot. 'They ingrew,' she said, and the atmosphere thawed for a time, becoming almost amiable. There was something Vicky wanted to ask Henrietta; on several occasions she opened her mouth to say it, and then stopped. But the minutes went by; at three o'clock Aunt Agnes came to the door and called them. They were sitting side by side on the hot stones – they looked round, and Vicky scowled. 'I suppose we're going,' said Henrietta, beginning to get up. Vicky pulled her down again. 'I want to ask you something.'

'Well, what?'

'Promise you'll tell me?'

'Well, how do you know I know?'

'They talk so much you'll have heard. They won't talk to me. Promise you'll tell?'

'I will if I know. Do hurry up.'

'Well, why do they all talk about my father like that?'

Henrietta went pink and took off her glasses. 'Like what?'

'What do you wear those beastly things for? You look all right without them. Well, you know what I mean, the way they talk; poor George, and all that. What do they mean?'

'Well, he's dead – I suppose they mean that.'

'They don't mean that. They say Poor Vicky. I'm not dead. And my aunts keep giving her sort of looks. Go on, tell me; you do know.'

'No, I don't. Shut up.'

Vicky took her wildly by the arm. 'I'll kill you if you don't tell me,' she said. Henrietta shook herself free. She remembered being told Vicky was not to be excited. 'You do know really,' she muttered. 'All right, I do know,' said Vicky calmly. 'Go on, tell me.' 'Vicky! Henrietta!' called Aunt Agnes from the quiet distant house. Vicky dug her fingers into Henrietta's boneless arm. 'Go on,' she said.

'It's because of your father. If you know all about it —'

'What about my father?'

'He went mad.'

Vicky let go and stared at her. 'He didn't,' she said at last.

'Well, he did. You said you knew.' Henrietta stared back; she held her glasses in her hand, short-sightedness gave her eyes a look of concern. She went on, 'His mother went mad, didn't she, when they were all children, so none of them could marry. My grandmother says your aunts were the prettiest girls she ever saw. They aren't very pretty now, are they? And your father married all of a sudden, ages afterwards, and they

were all awfully upset, and then he went mad and died. But I don't suppose it's catching,' she added kindly.

Vicky made no answer; her black slippers rattled on the stones and she ran up to the house. Henrietta followed uneasily, hoping she was not going to say anything about it while they were still there. Vicky did not: she shook hands with Mrs Casey and politely said Goodbye to the ruby brooch. 'I have so enjoyed it,' said Mrs Casey to Aunt Agnes. 'Such a lovely talk, the first real talk we've had for twenty years. You simply must come over to Longhurst soon. You will, won't you?'

'We should like to,' said Aunt Agnes, plainly not meaning to do anything of the sort. Henrietta and Mrs Casey, waving their hands out of the windows like fins, swam away down the smooth road in their Austin Ten.

Instead of going upstairs to change into her shorts Vicky followed the aunts into the drawing-room and sat down on her stool in front of the needlework firescreen. She twined her arms round her knees and looked up at them. 'Aunt Agnes,' she said, 'did my father really go mad?'

Their three battered faces turned a greenish colour in the faint light, but there was no pause. Aunt Agnes said in the same tranquil voice that she had used to Mrs Casey, 'Who has been telling you that, Vicky? Henrietta? She is a stupid gossiping child and we are ashamed of her. Your father was very ill before he died and it affected his brain, but he was never mad. He was not mad at all.'

'She said that was why you and Aunt Violet and Aunt Marianne never married.'

As if she were going to start singing some mournful aria, Aunt Agnes gently clasped her hands and held them in front of her. 'Vicky, there is nothing for you to worry about. We hope you will grow up and get married like everyone else, normally. Your aunts and I —' she looked at her sisters, '– your aunts and I never married, it's true. But that was not because of anything to do with the question at all. That was because,' she said clearly, and gestured with her linked hands, 'nobody ever asked us.'

'No,' said Aunt Marianne, 'you see, Vicky, nobody asked us.'

And Aunt Violet, in a voice as desolate as an echo's, murmured, 'Never.'

THE HORSE

At six o'clock Mrs Sedley ran out to answer the bell, but it was only her child, who had been to tea with another child from school. 'Oh, it's you,' she said. 'I didn't think they'd be punctual. *Wipe your shoes.*'

'Who?' said Angela. She bent her ankles over, shuffled backwards on the sides of her feet.

'You always come back from Susan's looking as if you ate off the coal-shed floor – wash quickly, now, and leave the basin *clean*. And change your —'

'Who?'

'And rinse it off, don't wipe it on the towel. Alingham and the Kendalls are coming in for sherry.' Ironing out her new dress of dark-red wool with her fingers, as if she had lumbago, Mrs Sedley turned to the doorway and looked critically at her sitting-room. When she put it into words in her mind, a habit that was growing on her since her first article had been accepted three weeks before, it sounded delicious. '"A bright fire burned in the hearth,"' she said to herself, '"the lamps were lit" – no, that sounds like paraffin; "light glowed through the pleated shades on the pale-green walls and ceiling, the

petunia curtains were drawn back, and through the windows in the blue dusk, behind the bare trees, was a glimpse of Chelsea Hospital and the silent stretch of the river."' Mrs Sedley shook her head in a dissatisfied way. Six feet of the Thames, however silent, could hardly be called a stretch; every fifth word seemed to be The, and the essence of her sitting-room remained elusive. Even the room itself sometimes troubled her, when she thought about it, with an indefinite wrongness. It looked like one of those rooms with a wall missing in an Exhibition of English Craftsmanship and Design. Mrs Sedley often took books and magazines from the impeccable shelves and mauled them about to give an unconvincing air of homey disorder, or left pieces of embroidery around or even Angela's stockings, but she never succeeded in making it look like anything more than the same room thrown open to the staff while the Exhibition closed for lunch. Now she took out *English Social History* and threw it on the settee. It lay there self-consciously. The cover was the wrong colour anyway, so she put it back and found a book that was the right shade and laid it open and face downwards. At this point, Angela came in, carrying her attaché case.

'*Don't* tell me you're going to make a mess with your homework,' Mrs Sedley howled irrationally.

'I'll do it in the corner. I've got to DO it,' said Angela, injured.

'How can you expect to concentrate when we're all talking? Besides, you'll – can't you take it in the bedroom? You can have the electric fire.'

'I don't want the electric fire. It only warms my knees.'

'Well, you're not —' The bell rang. 'You're not going to stay up half the evening doing it when they've gone,' said Mrs Sedley, ironing and patting and rattling out to open the door. Angela stuck out her lip and took inky exercise-books from the case. She unscrewed her fountain-pen and shook it over the Sheraton table and blotted up the three spots with the edge of her navy tunic. At the top of a cleanish page she wrote slowly, THE HORSE.

When the sherry was poured out, Mrs Sedley sat at one end of the couch and Alingham at the other, and between them lay the book. Alingham was talking about Paris where he had just spent a month. He held his glass in the careless way admired by Mrs Sedley, and ran the other hand, with a cigarette between the two middle fingers, over the straight, light gauzy hair that swept back to the nape of his neck. Kendall leaned against the Adam mantelpiece, waiting to talk about Bolzano where he had just spent a fortnight. Kit, his wife, sat on the floor wearing culottes and red knitted socks and staring in a detached way through her hair at Alingham. Kendall had hardly started on Bolzano when Mrs Sedley became aware that Alingham had picked up the book to read its title. As soon as he put it back, she read it herself, upside down, and saw that it was *Forever Amber*. Confused, appalled, she looked up and met his eyes, which were light blue; he smiled rather sweetly. Mrs Sedley did not know what to do, but since Kendall went on talking she had no choice, she could only listen and say nothing, and in ten minutes or so of telling herself not to be silly she recovered. She poured out

more sherry and the conversation began to loosen up and she was drawn into it.

She felt always that she had no real right to be there; her one article in a woman's magazine would not change into a square the triangle of Kendall, an established writer and critic, and Alingham who had written three intelligent novels, and Kit who successfully painted and could talk about existentialism. Still, she thought, everyone's got to start. The idea of having set her foot on the ladder made her feel warm and clever. Her room was not now an exhibit but a setting; she looked round it with temporary pride and saw in the far corner her child, a lamp at her elbow, inkstains on one cheek, her round eyes fixed unblinking on Alingham who was holding forth about Scandinavian drama. Mrs Sedley craned round a vase of flowers. Two words were written at the top of Angela's page; the rest was blank.

'Angela,' she said in a kind of shrieked whisper, 'do get on.'

Alingham stopped talking; the company's attention was switched to the corner. 'Are you doing your homework?' said Kendall.

Angela dived under the table in pursuit of a foot, leaving only her head in view, murmuring 'Yes'. Mrs Sedley's face wore the apprehensive pride of a mother whose child has to recite at the school concert. 'She's been out to tea,' she said. Kendall took no notice, but asked Angela politely what she was doing.

'Sit *up*,' said Mrs Sedley. Angela came to the surface, pulled off one hair-ribbon and re-tied it just below her ear on the end of a plait. She said, 'I'm writing an essay on The Horse.'

'Are you stuck?'

'She hasn't started,' said her mother.

'Do they still do that?' said Kit in her slow, deep drawling voice. 'They always did. The Horse, and How I Spent My Holidays, and A Day In The Life of a Penny.'

'Well, they do offer some scope,' said Alingham.

'Not to children. In the Third Form there *is* only one essay on The Horse. It begins, The Horse is a very useful animal,' said Kit.

'That would never do,' Kendall said. 'Angela must be different. We have three professional writers on the spot, and one of them is her mother, and if we can't explain to her how to write an essay on The Horse that will knock the Third Form unconscious, we might as well retire. First of all, Angela, you must think what aspect of the subject you are going to deal with, you see.' Mrs Sedley was almost knocked unconscious herself at being referred to by Kendall as a professional writer. With eyes grown large and dark, and an expression first stunned, then awed, then delighted (after all, I *did* earn ten guineas by writing), she looked from the intelligentsia in the firelight to her child's face smiling painfully in embarrassment and pleasure. It's nice of them, she thought; it will help her so much; I do want her to be something clever when she grows up.

'The aspect I remember best,' said Kit, 'is the one from underneath when you've just fallen off.'

'At my school,' said Alingham, 'we used to quote a great deal. It fills up space.'

'"I know two things about the Horse. And one of them is rather Coarse,"' said Kendall.

Mrs Sedley murmured, 'I don't really think —'

'The point is,' said Kendall, 'you must have an angle. That's quite essential. It's no good making a lot of statements about horses that everyone else will make too; such as the fact that machinery has largely taken their place, or that some have their tails cut short, or that there are wild ones on Dartmoor. You've got to be original – you've got to shoot a line and keep on shooting it. You could, for instance, write about nothing but how awful horses are, how they step on your toes and always know whether you can ride or not and always start moving off as soon as you've got one foot in the thing.'

'But I *like* horses,' said Angela, horrified.

'But that isn't such a good angle,' said Kit. 'It doesn't matter in the least what you really think, you know.'

'But if she wants to be pro-horse,' said Kendall, 'and there's no reason why she shouldn't, she could take the line that all machinery should be blown up and we should go back to conditions of the eighteenth century, only, of course, on a larger scale because of the increase in population. Millions and millions of horses, think of it – think of Piccadilly.'

'They wouldn't breed fast enough.'

'But nor do cars; one would put one's name down with a good mare, you know, instead of Austin's or Standard's; and horses would have to be nationalised, and licensed, and all the roads would have to be broken up because of their hooves.'

'And agriculture would benefit enormously,' said Kit, 'only of course it would be trampled flat.'

'Do have some more sherry,' said Mrs Sedley. 'I hope you're remembering all this,' she said to Angela.

'Perhaps it's a little complicated for the Third Form,' said Kendall. 'Perhaps what would go down better would be an exercise in good clean fun, you know, about how to get on facing the head or pointed end, and what part of the saddle to hold on to. Or you could analyse the effect horses have on horse-lovers, or the fact that while most horse-lovers love dogs, very few cat-lovers love horses, and find out why; it's something to do with fawn check tweed, I think. Or again –'

'You confu-use the child,' Kit drawled.

'He talks too much,' said Alingham to Angela in his very clear, plaintive voice, 'but what he is trying to tell you is quite right – the important thing in an essay is to have a fresh approach, to write something that hasn't been written before and that could only be written by you. It doesn't have to be long, or learned, or full of big words, but if you can make people say "I never thought of that", it will be a good essay. You mustn't make a list of all the facts about horses, because that would be dull, but you must think of one aspect of the subject, as Kendall says, and write about that. Do you see what we mean?'

'Like the way horses work for nothing,' said Angela. She was pink-faced, but pleased.

'That would do very well. Perhaps we expect too much from horses; if you believe that, you must say so.'

'"The Horse – It Works – Its Duty Never Shirks,"' said Kendall. 'You could put that in at the beginning. Should horses be encouraged to strike? Should they have a union, an insurance scheme, a pensions system? Ask the Third Form that.'

'You take everything too far,' said Alingham. 'But there is the point, Ursula, I mean Angela, whether we have the moral right to use animals as labourers at all. They have no choice; they're conscripted whether they like it or not and they can't ask for holidays or shorter hours or better conditions, and perhaps because of that we shouldn't use them. Could you write on those lines, do you think?' Alingham's gaze, his attitude, were anxious and intent; Mrs Sedley saw that with more feeling than Kendall he really cared about Angela's essay and wanted to help. She was surprised, and suddenly in spite of his three novels he no longer overawed her. In not quite the same way, the Kendalls had been nice, too; Mrs Sedley, smiling round at her sitting-room, thought how kind it was of all of them to help Angela and how pleased Miss Thoreau would be with Angela's essay. She imagined Miss Thoreau saying in the staffroom, It's a quite exceptional piece of work, but, of course, her mother writes, doesn't she? Stifling the realisation that Miss Thoreau had almost certainly not seen the article and that Angela's last ranking for Composition had been B Minus, Mrs Sedley happily filled up glasses and turned half her attention to Kendall, who was talking about pre-war German films. What with the sherry, and the warmth, and their kindness to Angela, she almost wept at their departure. 'Do come again, any time,' she begged them, and Kit said, 'You must come and have a drink with us. I'll ring you up, shall I?' Mrs Sedley, when she shut the door on them, leaned against it and breathed deeply. She was In.

Angela in the corner wrote slowly. Her tongue was out, her legs entwined with those of the chair. Mrs Sedley began smoothing cushions, picking up glasses, emptying ashtrays, turning her room back into an Exhibit. Angela went on writing. 'Well,' said Mrs Sedley at last, 'I hope it's going to be a really good essay. I hope you realise how nice it was of them to help.'

'They kept talking about Third Form. I'm in Four B.'

'Well, how could they know that? You quibble so. Wasn't Alingham kind?'

'He called me Ursula,' said Angela, writing.

'Oh, don't be ridiculous. Anyway, it was only a slip. Can you remember all the things he said? If you can't, you'd better ask me.'

'I can.'

'– Thank you.'

'Thank you.'

'Well, don't hurry it, but when you've finished you'd better go to bed. It's getting late.' Mrs Sedley picked up the tray and carried it into the eight-by-six kitchen. The essay took a long time; finally, though reluctantly, she had to start badgering.

'Oh, all *right*,' said Angela. 'You *said* I wasn't to hurry. I've done it, anyway.'

'I hope it's good.'

'Well, it's awfully *long*.'

When her child was at last in bed and asleep, Mrs Sedley prowled in and fetched the attaché case from the floor under the dressing-table. She felt she had to see, as a mother and a writer, the beginnings of Angela's literary blossoming. She

sat down in Alingham's place by the fire and opened the exercise-book. At the top of the page a blot had been doodled into a vase with handles. Mrs Sedley frowned, and began to read:

THE HORSE

The horse is a very useful animal. Horses were used then more than they are now, it still pulls milkarts and people ride them. The horse was used in battles before there were tanks. There were no cars or busses so people rode about on them. In Dartmoor there are wild ones called Ponies. Some horses have their tails cut off or some are plated with straw. Horses are used for hunting and raceing and pulling carts and ploghs, but some ploghs are horsless, they are called tracters. The horse is a very nice animal. They eat hay. horses like apples and sugar. Some bite and kick but they are very kind, and it works hard. I do not know any more about horses so I will cloase.

Mrs Sedley sighed. She put the book back in the case, which contained also a half-eaten apple, a piece of barley-sugar covered with fluff and india-rubber sediment, and some skeleton leaves. She leaned back with her feet up and lit a cigarette dispiritedly. This was the moment to begin another article. Mrs Sedley thought for several minutes about beginning another article; then she fetched herself a glass of sherry, and with a faint air of guilt picked up *Forever Amber*.

INIGO

After the soldiers and the strangers had left the town, and after she had lived there through war and peace for nine years without getting to know more than half a dozen people, Harriet fell in love. The soldiers went, leaving traces behind them – a way of dancing, a way of speaking, an indefinite number of white babies and three black ones, and a kind of coma settled on the town again, and the babies grew into children and were sent to school, and then this thing happened to her.

Harriet did clerical work for the County War Agricultural Committee. The county was small, the county town of a proportionate size, and the Committee shared with the Forestry Commission, the Women's Institute and various other activities, a little Palladian mansion that had been built by Inigo Jones for the Corvillon family. It was not an exciting job, but Harriet had a respect for architecture and its setting gave her the greatest pleasure. She was not a native of the town; no nostalgia troubled her for the house's past, such as overcame the more aged WI members who had once played picquet and danced polkas with the now dead Corvillons and still saw

spectral Sheraton disparaging the ministerial deal. Harriet's desk was utilitarian, but she dealt with crop returns under gilded stars on the ceiling and thought it right that the house should work for a living too.

Out of office hours she lodged in Mrs Shellback's attic. Mrs Shellback was a little Cockney widow with three daughters; one was a typist, one in a shop, and the third at school. Where the Corvillons' house appealed as the flower of a single period, the Shellbacks' had the opposite charm of stark architectural lunacy; Harriet often diverted herself with research and guesswork on the toy, wrought-iron balconies arguing Regency with an Edwardian glass porch, the medieval castellations on an anonymous turret, the Victorian gables, the vaguely Georgian windows and the chewed beams in her attic roof. The house missed disaster by a coat of whitewash, which somehow held it together; its size – for it was very small – gave it the melancholy, animated air of a folly. Most of the garden was in the front, an oblong of lawn with a path of pink crazy paving and a pear tree. Mrs Shellback grew her vegetables out of sight behind the toolshed. 'Must 'ave a nice bitter lorn to sit on,' she said firmly. Harriet thought this was a tenet of respectability rather than a practical objective, for Mrs Shellback was never seen to sit down anywhere. She was the original Human Dynamo. The inside of her house was an unconscious parody of its exterior – ferns on bamboo tables fought with Utility tables and George the Third chests in a restricted space for the eye's attention. Harriet's own furniture in the attic looked, by comparison, almost indecently naked. The ceiling sloped to within three feet of the floor. At

one end a round window like a porthole overhung someone's large garden, and at the other, an oblong one with a kind of gargoyle above it opened on to a balcony. The balcony held a deckchair, but only if the casements were shut.

Between Mrs Shellback's house and Inigo Jones's there ran a narrow lane with on one side a high wall of dark-red brick and on the other a row of slummy but not unattractive cottages, all different shapes and sizes, all about a hundred and fifty years old, with no front gardens. Across the end of the lane reared the white Palladian gateway. It took Harriet three minutes to walk from her work to her lodgings. She disliked canteens, and so every day she came home and sat reading in the attic while she ate her lunch.

One morning in early February, a false spring poured untimely sunlight on the town; the sky was Chinese blue, scraps of paper eddied on a warm breeze down the lane. Harriet, wearing with the inbred unconscious pessimism of the English a mackintosh, came down Mrs Shellback's pink path and out of her respectable gate. She looked neat, fresh and indifferent; indifferently she walked past the cottages, their doors open on stone flags, rag mats, a red tablecloth and a thinly ticking clock. They invited no attention but the sun's, and Harriet was not moved to the incivility of looking inside. Halfway down the lane she skirted an unwonted pram. A pram was not like an open door; vaguely, in passing, she inspected its contents. Two cottages further on the urge was irresistible; she went back to have another look. On a cotton pillow, covered to the ears with a rug that seemed to be knitted of brown twine, lay a minute transparent baby. Its eyes were

shut; veins as faint as the tracings of a blue pencil were drawn on its eggshell skull, a feather of hair like dust blurred the line of its head on the hardly whiter cloth. Harriet stared at it disbelievingly. The cottage door was closed, squalid curtains were drawn across the windows; only an ungroomed pram seemed to connect the baby with reality. She looked for several minutes, and finally walked up the lane and through the white pillars of the gateway. All the morning, dealing with forms under the classical ceiling, she kept thinking what a ridiculous, touching, insubstantial baby it had been.

When she went home to lunch, and when she returned at a quarter to two, it was still there. It had not apparently even moved; Harriet, prodigiously inexperienced with babies, began to wonder if it were dead. Each time she passed she hovered incredulous over the pram, looked with a touch of anxiety and accusation at the silent cottage. In a dusk already cold, the day's work finished, she hurried out of the gates into the lane and saw the pram still where it had been since the morning. Now convinced the baby had died of hunger and exposure, Harriet unwillingly prepared to beat up the inmates of the cottage, and failing an answer from them, the police. But when she reached it she saw that someone had moved it on to its other side. Another infinitesimal profile of a button and a closed eye, another blue vein and feather of dust confronted her; even Harriet knew that nothing of that size could turn over by itself. Staring back over her shoulder, half-reassured but still uneasy, she went on down the lane.

In the attic she drew curtains over the dusk and lit the gas fire, and pottered around washing and tidying and changing

her shoes till Mrs Shellback came clattering up with a tray. Harriet was not sociable, she talked to strangers with difficulty, but with Mrs Shellback she had a firm friendship that she would have been desolated to lose. At her job she worked efficiently in a shell of reserve. Unless she went to the one cinema, she spent all her evenings in the attic, reading, writing or listening to music in her own ordered company. Mrs Shellback was what might be called the light relief of Harriet's existence; and since Harriet had reached the age of thirty-two without any relief lighter than that provided by her landlady, it must be admitted that she was indeed of a serious turn of mind.

When Mrs Shellback came up with the tray, Harriet said to her, 'There's a very small baby outside a cottage down the lane. It's been there all day and it's still there now, in a pram, I mean, and it doesn't seem to move or anything. I hope it's all right.'

Mrs Shellback put down the sausages and sprouts, happy to argue on anything from infant welfare to the Trans-Siberian Railway. 'That's the modern way, that is,' she said, 'feed 'em and wash 'em and drop 'em in the pram like they was 'ot. Scientific training, they calls it. Scientific 'ell. I don't 'old with it. Don't 'urt no kid to 'ave a bit of attention, on and orf.'

'It's nearly dark,' said Harriet.

'Gets fed at six, most like. That's another thing, feed 'em on the dot you 'ave to now. Mine got theirselves fed when they bawled for it, and it don't seem to 'ave done 'em no 'arm. Anyway, you got no call to worry. Trust all them blarsted gyppos down the road to 'ave their bloody noses stuck on the

windows, minding other people's business.' Mrs Shellback had a ferocious contempt for the local population; she refused to fraternise.

Harriet was relieved about the baby; but all the same she wrote an overdue letter to a cousin she disliked, and went out to post it at eight o'clock. The pram had gone. She returned to a book and a concert, and forgot about it. That was the last time she went to bed ignoring the baby's existence.

After that, like a cancer or a drug, it projected itself into her life. If it had been a moderate-sized baby, one fresh and cared-for like the average child, she would have passed it by with disinterested benevolence; but its minuteness, its air of fragility and of being unwanted, pushed outside into the public eye and there left and perhaps forgotten, enslaved her first with a social conscience and then with a more subjective anxiety. When she first saw it, it could not have been more than eight or nine days old. Passively indifferent, it simply lay where someone invisible had put it, unable even feebly to move its covered hands, to adjust the brown twine rug or the angle of light in its eyes. If it was too cold or too hot it cried, but no one heard it. Milk that it dribbled on the pillow damped its cheek; no one came to put clean cotton under its head.

Harriet had never had anything to do with babies. Common sense told her that this one, since it remained alive and even began perceptibly to grow, was being fed by the invisible someone and therefore had prospects not quite as dim as those of thousands of babies in Europe and Asia who were not being fed at all. But such a comparison pointed to

no more than a continued existence rather than a premature end; and here Harriet asked herself whether the advantages of existence outweighed the case for early oblivion, since it seemed pitiably little that the baby had to look forward to. Four times every day she gazed into its direly utilitarian pram; seeing no face ever peering from the cottage window, hearing no sounds of life behind the door, she spent first a minute and then three or four in her conscientious hovering, and soon grew more bold and began to tilt the hood against the sun or arrange the string rug as shelter from a wind. Seeming resigned to its fate, the baby rarely cried. After a week or two, it showed signs of an elemental awareness, lying sometimes awake on its side with one eye of milky indigo opened on the light antithesis of dark, waving one starfish hand outside its envelope, or grimacing in its sleep. That her mind should be always occupied with someone else's baby would have seemed incredible to Harriet a month ago, and remained even now unreal. But her concern persisted.

She said no more to her landlady, because the more Mrs Shellback ran down the gyppos (and this she was always happy to do on the least provocation) the more uneasy Harriet became about the baby's fate. Mrs Shellback, however, never forgot a remark. One rainy evening when Harriet came in (having lingered over the baby, implored it not to cry, tipped the water from a mackintosh pram-cover like a sheet of cast-iron and retreated desolate from its wailing) she screamed from the kitchen her usual formula when the weather was bad: "Ave a cupper, duck? It's 'ere 'ot on the 'ob.' Harriet went into the firelight, taking off her raincoat; her short, dark hair

curled with damp; she had a distracted look. 'I seen your biby today,' said Mrs Shellback, passing her on the way to the teapot. She stuck out her neck as she tore by and stared closely at Harriet, and Harriet said nothing.

'It's a shime,' said Mrs Shellback invitingly, 'bless its 'eart. On yer mind, ain't it?'

'Nobody seems to look after it.'

'Nobody don't want 'em when they comes without bein' arsked. Not 'aving got no father, see.'

'You don't know it hasn't got a father,' said Harriet, stung into defence.

'Ain't many round 'ere *as,*' said Mrs Shellback libellously. She stopped skirretting round the kitchen and watched Harriet. 'Glad to get rid of it, I daresay, if anyone'd 'ave it.' After a pause she added, 'Nothink like 'aving a biby in the 'ouse.' She allowed Harriet no pause for reflection; instead, she began to talk about something else. Harriet finished the tea and went upstairs to the attic. When she was shut into solitude, and only then, she retrieved Mrs Shellback's remarks from the store of her mind.

On the Sunday she went out before two o'clock and walked with determination up and down the lane; up to the Palladian gateway past the pram, back to the hybrid house, up and down again, looking at the dusty torn curtains of the cottage, the door shut fast against intrusion. At twenty past two she saw over her shoulder a woman come out and pick up the baby. Brown rug and all she lifted it up and disappeared again, its head rolling helplessly. She was an oldish woman with tails of grey hair and shuffling carpet slippers. Harriet went on

walking up and down. Twenty minutes later the act was
repeated in reverse, and she returned to the house in anger
and frustration. She discovered in herself the emotion of
someone whose property is being pawed by someone else.
This rather alarmed her.

With touching confidence in existence the baby grew;
every day it was a little larger, less fragile and indifferent, less
bound in the blank sleep of the newly-born. The veins were
still blue under the thickening down on its skull, its infinitesimal hands still useless in their moving, it did not yet ask
the ungiven affection, but for its empty future it began to look
a degree more equipped. The degree was none the less so
small that Harriet was not reassured. If anyone had told her
she felt more than anxiety and a social responsibility for the
baby she would have argued and denied it, till one morning
she found it awake, and both its ink-blue eyes focused on her;
in idiotic surprise it stared at someone who was there looking
at it for no reason except interest; in immediate response,
it smiled. That toothless undemanding reaction finished
Harriet. The baby was no longer a grounds for conscience; it
projected itself into intimacy.

Thus adopted, Harriet went on her way disturbed. Now
she began to wonder what was its sex and what its name.
About the former there was nothing she could do, but as for
its name she thought it unlikely that its owners, if they had
troubled to give it one at all, had risen any higher than Albert
or Rosie. Harriet winced at the idea of both. She went through
the elegant gateway and the conviction came to her that it was
a boy. She looked up at the house's façade, the classical pillars

almost transparent in the light – the house and the baby shared her pleasure, the past I Am of the one and the future I Could Be of the other. It must be a boy; its name must be Inigo.

Now with its title and its achieved humanity the baby filled her mind to the exclusion of her work. She was not pleased to find Marston in the office that day. A large part of his time was spent going from farm to farm while Harriet, his admirable machine, dealt with the results. Marston's feelings towards Harriet were much the same as Harriet's towards her typewriter; perversely, he found her efficiency a thought off-putting; unlike the junior typists, who were too human to be good, she was too good to be human. He was a widower, forty years old, with green eyes and a string of agricultural degrees. Harriet liked him because he had an orderly brain.

They worked together most of the morning. Towards midday, while Harriet was typing out a letter, Marston lit his pipe and looked at her, sensing something different to which he could not put a name. When the letter was finished and signed, he said tentatively, 'It's none of my business, I know; but I think you have something on your mind.'

Harriet stared at the typewriter; ready to deny intrusion, she felt, nevertheless, a desire for advice less prejudiced than Mrs Shellback's, and Marston was sensible. She said at last, 'I'm worried about a baby.'

Marston raised his eyebrows. Harriet blushed. 'It's some-one else's,' she said.

'Go on.'

He listened in silence. '. . . So you see,' said Harriet at the end, 'it started as pure interference on my part, but now it's something more personal. That makes it worse, I think.'

'Well, no,' said Marston. 'I think it makes it better. What do you want to do about it?'

'I'd like to adopt it,' said Harriet. She looked faintly astonished.

Marston's reactions were simple; he was vastly intrigued. Already Harriet had an ordinary animation, an appearance of suffering from doubts and emotions like everyone else, that he had not known she was capable of. He was moved by her description of the baby, and it touched him that anxiety about a stranger's child should be enough to change her thus quickly from a machine into a woman. 'Why don't you go and see them?' he asked.

'That's what I should do, I know,' said Harriet, 'but I don't believe I have the courage. I don't like talking to people. Suppose they threw a bottle at me or slammed the door in my face – and then I'm afraid that even if they don't want it they wouldn't want to let it go. People are supposed to feel like that about their own children, aren't they? If that happened, I couldn't bear seeing it every day, getting dirtier and more uncared-for, and beginning to *know* about it. That's the worst part. Now it's so small it just has to accept things, but I don't like to think of later on. I ought to go and talk to them, I do realise.'

'It's not uncommon,' said Marston, 'keeping what you don't want rather than letting someone else have it. On the

other hand, it's got to be fed and clothed after a fashion; it's bound to be an expense to them.'

'My landlady insists it's illegitimate.'

'Well, it probably is, but I can't see that its parentage matters from that angle. You have to take a risk on heredity anyway, but environment is so important that it seems to me a risk worth taking. What about your job?'

'Oh, I'd keep on, of course. Mrs Shellback is dying to look after it in the daytime; in fact,' said Harriet, 'she started it all by hinting I should try to adopt it. She has three children of her own who are an excellent advertisement for her, but they're nearly grown up. And I could afford to give it a good education; I've saved up quite a lot of money. I do wish I could have it.'

'Look,' said Marston to his own surprise, 'I'm used to dealing with people who don't want to see me. I'll go and deal with the baby for you, if you like.'

Harriet looked at him with candid amazement. She said finally, 'It would be the greatest help – I should be very grateful; but I can't see why you should do all this for me. I was being inefficient already, if it hadn't been for that you wouldn't have noticed, and I haven't anything to do with the baby yet.'

'One must take the long view,' said Marston.

Harriet opened the Gothic door in the Edwardian glass porch that same evening and heard Mrs Shellback milling around in the kitchen, bawling when her lodger's footsteps sounded, 'Want a cupper, duck?' Harriet went in and leaned

against the dresser, and Mrs Shellback stopped milling and fixed her with a beetle stare. 'Wotever's 'appened?' she said. 'You don't 'arf look different. Not got the sack, 'ave you? 'Ere's the tea.'

'Mrs Shellback,' said Harriet solemnly, taking the cup, putting it down and forgetting it as if it had never been, 'I'm going to adopt the baby. If I give you another pound a week will you look after it while I'm working and do its washing?'

'Gawd 'elp us!' said Mrs Shellback with a piercing scream. 'Cor,' she added, subsiding, 'I never thort you'd do it. Cor, I ain't 'arf glad. A pound a week 'ell; I don't want nothink for it – cor, I'll look arter it like it was me own. When're we goin' to 'ave it?'

'In a week or two, I hope; things have to be arranged first, and I'll have to get ready.'

'Gawdstrewth, ducks,' said Mrs Shellback, 'did you 'ave to go and knock 'em up? Wot 'appened?'

Harriet told her about Marston. 'The old woman's its grandmother (you were right, it's illegitimate) and the daughter's away all day, working in a factory. They were going to try and get it in a Home when it was six months, and can you imagine, she goes out all the morning charring and leaves it in the road alone. Can you *imagine* – and I didn't tell you, it's a boy.'

'Well, wot a bit of luck,' said Mrs Shellback, 'always wanted a boy, I did, 'ad a bellyful of girls, three and one miss wot was a girl, too. You won't 'ave to buy no cot for it, neither, 'cos I got mine in the shed, ain't 'arf a nice one when it's all cleaned up, and I got all me nappies, too, and things wot I was

savin' for me grandchildren; carn't see no signs of none yet,
and they can take their charnce when they does come: missed
the bleedin' bus, they 'ave. Wotcher goin' to call 'im?'

'Inigo,' said Harriet.

'Cor,' said Mrs Shellback.

Harriet went on leaning against the dresser and thinking
of the baby, of its toothless smile, its round, feathered head
on the dirty pillow, of the string rug and the door closed
fast on an empty house. Mrs Shellback went on rushing and
dabbing distractedly round the kitchen, muttering, 'I'm that
worked up I don't know where to put meself.' With her head
in the larder she was struck by another thought; she said, ''E's
a widower, ain't 'e?' But Harriet had gone; on the edge of the
table her untouched tea grew cold.

'I know 'e is,' said Mrs Shellback aloud to herself; like a
vacuum cleaner she swept up the cup in passing, and drank
it on her way to the sink.

It was not quite dark, but the lamp was alight in Harriet's
attic and the curtains drawn against the dusk. Though it had
always seemed to Mrs Shellback a cold half-furnished place,
white like a hospital and all that dark-blue striped stuff like
sacking on the chairs, now when for the first time in three
years she took up a tray laid for two she thought it looked
like a different room. The tray was heavy with an ambitious
meal; Mrs Shellback was doing her share in making sure
that Marston's first visit to see Inigo should not be his last.
From the darkness of the stairs she saw through the open door
the ring of lamplight enclosing Harriet and Marston on each

side of the fire, illuminating Harriet's new lacquer-red dress and Marston's lemon-yellow tulips in a white urn; beyond the light's compass, shut away by a thin screen, she looked through the bars of the cot at the baby asleep under a rug as pink as coconut ice, with a rabbit sewn in the corner. It slept quietly with a curled hand lying on each side of its head, under its round cheek a snowy pillow with a frill hand-worked by Mrs Shellback nineteen years ago. Muttering something with a pleased expression, she went in with the tray.

Back in the kitchen, Mrs Shellback for once sat down. She was feeling rightly complacent; out of nothing she had created a family, out of a surplus woman and an unwanted baby and a widower, by doing little else but hint. True, it was a family of a somewhat – so to speak – prefabricated nature, it was put together in the wrong order, the baby first and the marriage (on which she counted prematurely but with con- viction) last; but to Mrs Shellback's way of thinking it was none the worse for that. She sat still on the edge of the chair for six minutes, thinking smugly about her achievement; then she said out loud, 'Well, carn't 'ang around with me feet up like this. Won't do no good to the biby, this won't.' She got up and moved the kettle on the range to make tea; and leaving it to sing she went out to the sink and started on the next morning's washing.

THE TRAIN AND THE GUN

'You be back one o'clock sharp, see?' his mother had said to him. She shouted after him from the door: 'Joe! You hear?' The boy looked back and saw her standing half in sunlight, half in indigo shade, holding a red hand over her eyes, against the cottage whitewashed and picked clean as a bone by the gales, and the void around and behind. She sounded cross, but she did not look it; unspoken conspiracy held them together till his father came back to part them, time his authority, time the knife that cut their freedom in pieces. The knife hung over them, and at one o'clock it would fall. Joe had no watch; beatings and angers had taught him to recognise in some inward consciousness the passing of hours. When the children he played with called at him 'Hi, Joe! What's time?' he was never more than five minutes out, five minutes fast, perhaps, but never slow. Every day he got home when the long hand of the brass ship's clock was almost on the hour, guessing by the sun, the tides, the clock in his mind, leaving himself time only to turn a minute's stare of loathing on his father's back as he washed at the sink. When his mother put the dinner on the table out would come his father's silver watch.

The red thick hand holding it, the thick body, the red face under the thick red hair, were the subjugation of his mother, the authority that jellied her eyes and stopped her voice. She was cut off from Joe; she would not look at him or speak to him.

Now in the April morning as he swung on the gate they were free and relieved, and she called after him crossly only in pretence. Joe went whistling down the path's steps, scars of milky-red soil kicked by ascending feet in the turf. He turned the curve of the hill, out of sight of the cottage, leaving it squat and bleached and suspended on the edge of the void, the edge of the cliff. The path dropped down to the beach, but he left it and went across the unused slopes, and when it was hidden he knelt down and moved a stone from the entrance to a rabbit-hole. Behind the stone was a piece of dead bush, and behind the bush his father's old revolver which he had stolen from the junk in the attic. It was unusable, being broken; but stealing it and keeping it thus hidden gave him a sense of equality and revenge. He stuck it in the leather belt that kept up his shorts, and swaggered along the slope. Down on the sands below he saw Tom and the others, dwarfed, foreshortened, playing with a dead seagull which one of them swung by a wing. Their voices came up faintly, muted to a tune instead of a scream. He took the gun in his hand and began to swoop and dodge and run, crouching with an air of intensity towards the breast of the hill, looking melodramatically over his shoulder to the beach. Before he had tired of this he reached the place where his body resting had worn a pinkish smudge in the grass.

Over the second hill no one was in sight. There were no houses. The bay swept round the pale-red cliffs and the flat sea was spread on the sand like silk edged with three little lace frills. It was the same milky blue as the sky, but polished with light. Below the hillside where he lay a creek ran inland from the shore and across its head the railway line emerged for three hundred yards, ejected from one cliff only to be swallowed by the other. The last few yards were hidden by a bank a little higher than the lines but from his vantage-point he could see both tunnels, black mouths in the red flesh of the rock. The express was due at eleven fifty-five; the clock in his mind said twenty to twelve. There he lay waiting, as he waited every morning of the holidays instead of joining the others on the beach, lying on one elbow on the hillside with the revolver in his hand, in a half-conscious attitude lifted from a film. His hair was his mother's hair, limp and dark; the fluid length of legs and arms gave his square face in contrast an air of untimely maturity. He was thirteen. He lay on the grass in the sun and lived over again the pleasure of a year ago when his father had gone away for three days. Time had gone with him; Joe and his mother lived from departure to return in a sweet and sluttish trance, with a duster hung over the ship's clock, smearing dripping on bread when their unpunctual bellies asked for food and eating it standing up or lying on the cliffs. Where he lay now his mother had sat beside him to watch the train.

His interest in the train was not technical. The nearest station was thirteen miles away and he knew little about the mechanics of railways. The express was called the Coastal

Arrow; its speed, its streamlining, its engine encased like a blunt-nosed bullet filled him with repelled and fascinated awe. These emotions drew him from the beach to watch it in the impressive seconds of its passing, propelled with such violence like a long and reddish shuttle from cliff to pale-red cliff. Its use, the conveying of men and women at their wish and for their convenience, hardly entered his mind; in his abstract conception it was simply an infernal machine.

The sound came first from over the sea, faintly till the tunnel shut it off. Under the cliffs it began again with a different note. He put down the revolver and sat up, knowing like a hardened concert-goer each timbre and cadence of the approaching climax. As the trained ear of the listener to music detects a false note before its impact on the mind, so his ear caught it – the something wrong this time – even while his open eyes and mouth waited on the engine's eruption from the tunnel. It came out with an almost human scream. Always for a second or two the whole length was to be seen before the engine plunged into the farther cliff. But this time it did not reach it at all. In his ears, before his unbelieving eyes, the train disintegrated.

He knelt on the grass unmoving. There was a majestic and fearful slowness about the catastrophe; the deceptive serpentine whole now broke up into its component parts, and engine and carriages reared and fell, braked by their cumbrous weight, the engine lying overturned and slantwise to the line while the last coach was yet with sluggish grace descending on the embankment over the rocks. The percussion of impact and rending steel came to an end and with a ghastly likeness

to untuned strings the screams began. Then for the first time
he realised the train was full of people. His face changed; he
moved his tongue over his lips, knelt hesitating; picked up the
revolver and began to run down the slope.

When he came close to the wreck he saw that activity
had already begun. These were the victims, the unhurt, who
stood dazed and dishevelled or clambered out of the ruins.
It was the moment when no plan was yet conceived, when
chaos was a vacuum and no one knew quite what to do. In
his stained shorts, with the gun in his hand, Joe was the
Untouched and the Outside, the spectator on the scene. His
iron stomach was proofed against horrors; his eye, seeking
melodrama, turned inwards and saw himself the rescuer and
the leader, cutting away wood, breaking shattered glass
and dragging the injured one after another from the wreck.
Boy Hero of Train Smash in the papers; perhaps even a
medal. Taking no notice of a thin high wailing from the
nearest carriage, he decided to start with the engine-driver.
On the line, near the engine's twisted nose, he saw the cause
of disaster, the drift of earth and rock fresh as new blood from
the cliff and scarred and flattened by the impact. The engine-
driver was past needing rescue; that part of him which was
free indicated the condition of the rest, and Joe turned his
eyes back to the carriage. He climbed on top, directed by the
falsetto wails, which began thinly to shape a word. 'Agnes!
Agnes! Agnes!' they cried. Out of the tunnel ran an old man
swinging a lamp. Joe set one knee on the edge of a door,
thrust his face down to the gap in a broken window, drew it
back when another face swam up at him from the dusty limbo

of inside. 'Agnes!' it screamed at him; then dropping suddenly to a flat, tired, peevish tone, it said almost conversationally, 'my dog's underneath.'

Baffled, Joe shifted his kneehold and began to knock out the loosened edges of glass with the revolver butt; he had no reply; the conviction grew on him that more rewarding rescue work was to be done elsewhere, but having once started on Agnes he dared not leave. He cleared the window of splinters, peered into the compartment and reached down an arm. 'Agnes is underneath. My dog's underneath.' 'Well, I got to get you out first, see?' said Joe in the reasonable level tones one uses to a lunatic. A large female hand, cold and damp, clutched his in a disembodied and horrifying grip; scuffling sounds and the rending of cloth went on in the dusty gloom; 'no,' said the face, 'no, it's no use. You'll have to go and get some help.' Anger and embarrassment locked Joe's fingers on hers. 'There isn't any help,' he said. 'Come on; you bloody well try. Come on, now.' The clammy grip was like the hold of a vice. With more scuffling and rending the victim was at last heaved out, enveloping him in fur and mothballs and the acrid smell of fear and sweat. Her large pale face panted down towards Joe's. 'Now my dog; my poor little dog —' 'Goddam your dog,' said Joe; all at once he could not bear this woman any longer, coming between him and the headlines and medals; he would have liked to cram her back in the wrecked compartment. Turning his head away from her he took on an agile cinematic pose with the gun in his hand and looked round for more rewarding action.

Now he saw that he was not the only helper on the scene;

drawn like flies from nowhere to a piece of decaying meat, others had arrived by some means and were in their varying degrees of inefficiency trying to release the injured. Along the side of the embankment lay a row of victims, neatly placed but all the same untidy, whether alive or dead Joe could not see. A man passed him below the overturned carriage to which he clung, carrying with an air of resigned distaste someone's hand, which, hung from his fingertips, swung like a crab. He threw it under a wrecked sheet of steel, wiped his fingers and went on. Joe took no notice of the female he had pulled out; she sat heaped beside him and whimpered. The old man with the lamp, standing beside the engine, shouted in a kind of penetrating whisper and pointed to the hillside. Joe looked up, towards where he had been lying. Down from the skyline over the precipitous grass came the ambulances, scoring weals like blood where they skidded on the slope but coming always down and down in a direct line to take over the rescue. There were three of them. Joe climbed off the carriage and began to walk towards where they would stop.

Someone called him from his intention, shouting 'Hi!' from a pile of wreckage almost on the beach. He saw the head and shoulders of a young woman beckoning to him from a gap that had been a door. Joe hesitated; he told himself he had had a bellyful of rescuing women. But something more decisive and competent in her gesture drew him unwillingly, and he went over, the gun swinging from his hand, turning his back on the inviting ambulances and coming to a halt by the twisted wheel that stuck out of the scrap-heap level with his eyes. The young woman was round-faced, sleepy and gentle

in expression; her hair, which looked light from the distance, was now seen to be thick with dust; dust thickened her eye-lashes, her tweed jacket was torn down one arm. 'Come and give me a hand,' she said; 'come up here, can you? There's someone inside.' Joe stuck the revolver in his belt and climbed up the debris. 'Why do you carry a gun?' said the young woman, who seemed quite unruffled and almost amused; 'are you a gangster?' Joe scowled, seeing patronage in her half-smile; he would not speak. As a co-rescuer he liked her even less than as a victim. He looked down into the gap where she stood and saw a woman's legs, in torn stockings, shoeless, emerging from under shattered wood and the splintered back of a seat. 'I can't move it by myself,' said the girl, 'but it isn't quite jammed. It shifts, look. We might get it off if you can help. A gunman ought to be strong. Or ought he?' she said, screwing up her dust-fringed eyes in the sun and staring at him. 'Perhaps the gun does instead.' 'I got no ammunition,' said Joe furiously; his voice broke on the last word and increased his anger and shame. He caught hold of the pieces of wood and together they began to haul them out and throw them over the side. Between them, panting and heaving, they pulled away the broken seat and inspected what lay beneath. 'Oh well —' said the girl, looking away; she wiped her hands on a torn handkerchief and climbed down to the ground. Along the top of the wreck a man was crawling, stopping at every gap to peer inside. He shouted to them, 'Any more in here?' 'One,' she called back. 'One dead.' Joe scraped his sandal in the torn grass. The man looked down the shattered funnel of roof and seat, and shook his head. 'Mostly out now,'

he said. 'Anyway there weren't many. Mostly got out back the last station, and a bloody good thing too. Christ, what a mess.'

Drifting unobtrusively away from the girl, Joe watched one of the ambulances turn and start up the seemingly impossible slope. Up it went obliquely in curves, crawling, almost stopping on the turns, but always up, eventually reaching the skyline and disappearing from sight. A faint sense of anti-climax, of having failed to do more than help out one uninjured woman and uncover one dead one, sent him lingering and backward-looking in the direction of home. He had started up the hill before he remembered the time, and in the same thought as the time, his father. The clock in his mind had stopped; it gave no answer but late, late. He did not even care. Conscience and habit impelled him to walk more quickly, but now there was no fear to prod him with urgency and soon his pace slackened again. He took the gun from his belt and threw it in the air, catching it with practised dexterity first by the barrel and then by the butt. On the height above the creek, in the dustless salt air from the sea, his memory turned aside the scene of effort and rescue and the people broken in the wreck. He lay down where he had been lying before, and turning aside too the thought of time and his father, he began to remember only the exquisite pleasure and ecstasy of the moment when the train, before it reached the tunnel, had smashed and disintegrated into ruin.

A FINE PLACE FOR THE CAT

Twice a week the green van came to the village; on the same two days Mrs Miller was up at half past eight and leaning out of the sitting-room window. Her lank hair and her dirty and faded green casement curtains blew about in the wind, and out of the sitting-room window she leaned to watch the cats; for Mrs Miller, though she was indeed a fat slut and had no beauty and few virtues, felt strongly enough about cats to get out of her bed an hour or more early two days a week winter and summer; and no other passion she was capable of had anything but the opposite effect.

Mrs Miller did not often or consciously look at the fish man himself, and nor did any of the women who came out through their swinging gates with a dish in their hands and a leather purse. Mrs Miller watched the cats from her window, and the women, standing one or two at a time in the half-secure screen of the van's open doors, looked no higher than his hands weighing, than the herrings and mackerel, the scales and the lifting from the tray to their dish; more than capable he was of slipping a little herring from clean under their noses down to Mrs Rhys's Tab who yelled for it beside

his boots. If his attention were distracted for a moment the women would shoo and scuff at Mrs Rhys's Tab with their squashed slippers, and Mrs Rhys's Tab would curl round to the other side of the fish man's boots; and Mrs Miller would put out her tongue at the women from her window.

Neither Mrs Miller nor any of the women who came out to buy herrings and mackerel could have told you anything about the fish man, except: he likes cats; medium tall he is, and thin; he wears a brown suit and a blue apron, his hair is drab, or greyish; cats it is with him, all the time. The village, except for Mrs Miller, thought him mad. Mad in this way is anyone who gives to cats what he might sell to women.

On Tuesdays and Fridays when the green van came to the village the tom cat from the Seven Stars waited on the stone pillar at the end of the bridge. Down from the driving-seat climbed the fish man to open the doors at the back, and the Seven Stars' cat, already at his feet with its wide cheeks puffed wider, put one paw on his leg and opened its triangular mouth for the consumption of a whiting that the fish man wedged into it, head and tail drooping on either side. The whiting and the Seven Stars' cat went off like a rocket into the yard of the inn; the fish man, disinterested, weighed out plaice for the landlord. Beyond Mrs Miller's cottage, down the street, all the other cats waited at their gates.

All the other cats waited for the fish man and their whiting, in the early morning sun and the smell of breakfast and bees-wax and the all-important smell of fish; in the cottages the children sat moving their mouths ringed with milk, and from her window Mrs Miller watched the fish man drive past

her from the Seven Stars to the other cottages, to the church gates; from the church gates back down the street, to stop last of all at her door. Though she did not like fish she ate it for dinner on Tuesdays and Fridays, in her parlour which was dirty and faded like the green casement curtains and had a dark circle on the buff wallpaper where she leaned back when she had finished, with her greasy head against the wall, a Woodbine in the corner of her mouth and her own cat Henry on her knees hooking fishbones off the plate and chewing them one-sided on her stained cotton overall. He was an old cat; age after the fashion of age had taken away his good shape and by nature he was not intelligent; he did not even to Mrs Miller's eyes seem impressive, seem the sort of cat one would be proud to see sitting outside the gate waiting for the fish man; but she was fond of him. The fish man, looking at Henry teetering away behind a whiting, would say with an air of melancholy, 'Indeed it seems wrong for a cat to be old, Mrs Miller.' True, Mrs Miller thought; but she said, 'Well, fond of them you get, like.'

In the winter Henry died. Mrs Miller grieved over him and refused the offer of a bastard kitten from the Seven Stars; but the fish man's visits became meaningless talking of other people's cats and in time she began to think about getting another of her own. A great deal she thought about it, and saw herself with a beautiful and impressive cat like none of her neighbours', like no other cat in the village. The fish man leaned on her gate in the snow and said, 'When will there be another Henry, now, Mrs Miller?' 'Maybe soon, now,' said Mrs Miller, looking remotely up at the dark trees laced with white

against the dark sky, behind his head. She took her two herrings on a plate and went flapping and crackling in her broken slippers up the snowy path and into her parlour to light the fire. She put the herrings on the rug beside her and sat on her heels pulling out from behind the coal-scuttle the crumpled paper in which Friday's cod had been wrapped. But when it was in the grate the word CATS looked at her between the bars and she pulled it out again and smoothed it on her knee, the front page of *The Times*. Feeling in her overall pocket for a bent cigarette, she read:

Pedigree female Siamese kitten for sale, 4 months; house-trained; 3½ gns. carriage paid. Letchley, Elm House, Hastock, Shrops.

Mrs Miller, with an unlit Woodbine in the corner of her mouth, sat and stared at the empty grate, seeing in its crusted depths a firm picture of her front path and an elegant cat treading it like a heraldic creature; an elegant cat indeed it was that she saw in the grate, with quantities of smoky-gold fur like feathers and a tail like a dark-gold ostrich plume waving against the snow. Mrs Miller had never seen a Siamese cat in her life. She got up from the hearthrug, leaving the herrings, and went to look for her wicked husband's old typewriter because she knew she had not the sort of handwriting in which to order a pedigree Siamese cat. It was a short letter and took her most of the morning. When it was finished she put a coat on top of her overall and went out and took some money from her Post Office account and added some more from the housekeeping and bought postal orders for three and a half guineas. Then she stuck a stamp on the letter and went back and lit the fire.

'Well now, where is the new Henry, Mrs Miller?' said the fish man on Friday, leaning on the white-edged gate; and Mrs Miller looked up at the trees and said, 'Coming any day now. A new sort of cat I'm getting,' she said, staring up at the sky closing like a grey oyster-shell over the village; 'a valuable cat,' she said with a casual folding of her dirty overall round her neck against the cold wind. 'There's good news, Mrs Miller, indeed,' said the fish man; 'a Persian cat, is it?' 'No,' said Mrs Miller, 'not an old Persian. Something different in the way of a cat it will be; not till it comes will you see what sort of a cat it is.' 'I hope it comes fast,' said the fish man, 'for I can't wait to know.' 'Like enough by Tuesday,' said Mrs Miller. 'It's a she-cat,' she said over her shoulder as she flapped away up the path.

The letter came saying when the elegant new cat would arrive at the station. There was some furtive feeling in Mrs Miller that she must look impressive for such a cat's first view of her, and she put on her best blue costume and pearl earrings and the coat with a piece of fur, and combed her hair round her fingers and walked a mile through the snow to the station in black shoes with high heels. She sat half an hour in the waiting-room, for the train was late, but when it came in at last with the single carriage furred with a rim of smoky snow she shot into the luggage office and leaned against the counter like a lady while Mr Jones who did everything at the station brought in a bicycle and a wicker basket of hens

and a smaller basket like someone's picnic lunch. Mr Jones put the smaller basket on the counter and it gave out a most appalling howl; a howl in a minor key it was, to make your blood run cold. 'God save us,' said Mr Jones, stepping back into the bicycle, 'what is it in there, Mrs Miller?' 'A cat, it is,' said Mrs Miller uncertainly, and leaned forward to point out the label saying VALUABLE CAT tied to the handle. 'Indeed that is no cat,' said Mr Jones; 'cats mew. Let us have a look, now,' he said, and took hold of the strap with caution; but Mrs Miller, hypnotised by the howl, said quickly, 'No, Mr Jones; I will be taking it home with me now. What would we do if it got out?' Mr Jones shook his head and said, 'You should not be opening it at home with no man in the house; indeed, Mrs Miller, I should come and stand over it with the poker.' 'No poker will I have waved over my pedigree cat, Mr Jones,' said Mrs Miller, recovering her aplomb, 'and a cat it is for sure; I bought it out of the paper; it howls with fright from your old train.' And she picked up the basket firmly and went out to the snowy road; by the time she got home to the cottage she was reconciled to such strangeness in a cat's voice and could not without difficulty wait to open the basket and see this elegant exotic creature that was to have dark-gold feathery fur and a tail like an ostrich plume.

So she put the basket on the parlour table before even she had taken off her coat, and undid the label and the strap and the catch and threw back the lid; and then reeling towards the fireplace she went with a melodramatic gesture like someone in a play, and cried 'God help us!', knowing she had been sold for a fool and palmed off with some kind of monkey. Away

went Mrs Miller's visions of long gold fur and golden plumes; such a sense of embarrassment she had now, thinking of what the fish man would say, and the neighbours, and whether the creature would spring on her and howl, for she could see only the top half looking out of the basket. A creature it was for sure and not a cat, thought Mrs Miller; what cat has fur as flat as a skinned rabbit and a face as pointed as a piece of cheese and eyes as blue as china and squinting inwards to its nose? And what cat was called not Henry or Tab or Smut but Tulan Caprian of Hastock? Mrs Miller spelt it out on the label. Disbelievingly she went on staring, and so did Tulan; disbelievingly she said 'Puss . . . ?', and went back another step when Tulan climbed out of the basket on to the table; truly Mrs Miller would not have been surprised to see four green paws and a red tail with a fork on the end, and was hardly less taken aback by these thin legs like a Victorian dancer's in dark stockings and a tail no thicker it seemed to Mrs Miller (who had not even now entirely given up thoughts of ostrich plumes) than a piece of tarred string. 'Well, God save us, delirious I must be,' she said to herself, and put the kettle on the fire with one eye on Tulan. Tulan sat on the table with that tail curled round those feet, and presently gave a tentative amiable howl. Mrs Miller, jumping at the tenor key, quickly took a plate of fish out of the cupboard and edged it on to the brown plush cloth. 'Well,' she said under her breath, 'one queer-looking monster you are and no mistake.' She backed away to the kitchen and made herself a cup of tea, which was not really what she wanted, but the Seven Stars was shut.

Alone in the parlour, in a shell of lamplight and firelight away from the dark and snow outside, they spent the evening, Tulan confidently and Mrs Miller with a shocked distrust. Every time she looked at the azure squint, the dark thin legs, the dark-brown tail like a monkey's and the flat short fur the colour of pale oatmeal with a glitter like the sun on snow, she thought about what the neighbours would say and above all the fish man tomorrow morning. Tulan sat in front of the fire with her dark pointed ears pricked up, turning the nearer one towards Mrs Miller when she sighed or muttered, as if in politeness to lose no word of what she said. This was unnerving; Mrs Miller fell silent and smoked a chain of bewildered cigarettes. At half past nine she made herself another cup of tea and Tulan for the first time jumped into her lap, curling dark feet under a pale swansdown breast, and purring. At half past ten she could not be left alone and wild in the kitchen or the parlour for the night. She slept on Mrs Miller's bed.

Because of the fish man the alarm clock was set for a quarter past eight. Mrs Miller woke to see Tulan square in her line of vision and six inches from her eyes. She recoiled and got out of bed. At once she thought of the fish man and wished she were safe in solitude, his visit past; but she said to herself, 'I will have to get it over, and a nuisance it will be; indeed he is sure to laugh at the creature; but I will get it over and out of the way.' She put on her clothes and her messy faded overall, and went down with Tulan to the kitchen.

When the fire was lit she slopped into the parlour and looked out of the window. There the green van stood outside

the Seven Stars, and the black tom cat (a cat to reassure you after the what-you-will chewing the table-cloth fringe behind your back) was galloping off with his whiting between the red and snowy pillars of the yard entrance. All down the street the green van went, stopping and selling fish to the women who came out with white dishes and strawberry noses into the cold, stopping and giving fish to the fine ordinary cats that mewed as cats should and rubbed their properly furred and covered flanks against the fish man's boots; down the street it went to the church gates, watched with growing misgiving by Mrs Miller from between her stained and faded green curtains, turned round, and drove back to her cottage. Mrs Miller looked despairingly at Tulan, picked up the enamel dish and went out of the blistered door.

'Well, Mrs Miller, now,' said the fish man with his hand on the gate, 'will the grand new cat be here yet?'

Mrs Miller looked up at the trees. 'Well,' she said repressively, 'arrived it has for sure; but indeed it's not the sort of cat I expected. It's a great wonder to me,' she said with a rush, preparing him for the worst, 'that it passes for a cat at all.'

'Very sad that is, Mrs Miller, now, if it's not what you hoped,' said the fish man, 'but perhaps it's only she will not be feeling herself after the journey.'

'Oh no,' said Mrs Miller on a round note, thinking of the parlour table-cloth, 'she is feeling herself all right; her looks it is that are not like a proper cat's at all.' She tapped her fingers on the enamel dish and stared up at the trees in silence, but the fish man was looking over her shoulder at the door. He looked past her at the cottage and the open door, and cried with such an air of surprise that she was startled, 'Why, Mrs Miller,' he cried, 'why, she's a beauty!' Mrs Miller turned round and saw Tulan, seeming very small, treading with her dark-legged dancer's step up the snowy path, with her dark ears pointed to the breath of fish, her dark thin tail like a question-mark up from the pale thin line of her back; Mrs Miller looked at her and saw with a shock that she was a beauty indeed. Now all the other cats seemed gross and without shape. But she said nothing, only stared at Tulan and tapped her fingers on the enamel dish; and Tulan trod up to the fish man and gave her urgent howl.

The fish man was enchanted; he took her up in his arms and said, 'Why, Mrs Miller, this is the greatest beauty of a cat I've seen in a lifetime, for sure. God save us, Mrs Miller,' he said, 'were you telling me you were disappointed in a cat like this? What sort of a cat is it called, now?' 'It's a Siamese cat,' said Mrs Miller, caught out in the wrong opinion and a little cross, 'and a big cat I thought it would be with a great tail like feathers.' 'So help me,' said the fish man, 'will you look at the blue eyes? What would you want with a lot of fur and no bones? Losing her to me you will be, Mrs Miller, if she's not the cat you wanted.'

'Well, I do want her,' said Mrs Miller quickly; 'it's getting used to her is a matter of time.' She looked at Tulan and then at the fish man, and in a moment she laughed; meeting the fish man's eyes over Tulan's head like two people in a film over the head of a reconciling child, for the first time Mrs Miller impaled him with a direct stare and saw that his eyes were as blue as the cat's; and for his part the fish man thought, the

cat's eyes are not more blue than hers. Tulan breathed fish over his shoulder, and howled. 'Well, Mrs Miller,' he said, and turned to the van, 'we will see what the beautiful cat would like.' He picked up a whiting by its tail and held it over Tulan who embraced it like a monkey, and hanging on by claws and teeth was lowered through the air to the ground. Mrs Miller and the fish man stood in the snow and watched the whiting disappear faster than you could believe. With Tulan there was no doubt the fish man was a success. 'What does your husband say to such a cat, now?' he said suddenly. Mrs Miller opened her eyes as startled as if Tulan had asked instead; she had not believed him capable of talking about anything but cats and fish and the weather. 'That I couldn't tell you,' she said, 'for he's not here.' 'In the Forces he would be, I expect,' said the fish man; and Mrs Miller said, 'Very likely, indeed, if they are not too particular; three years it is since he set eyes on me and I would be sorry if I saw him again.' 'That's a sad thing for you, Mrs Miller,' said the fish man, 'and grieved I am to hear it, but we all make mistakes.' Mrs Miller looked at the high trees, and after a pause she said, 'Well, I will be going in now.' 'Well, you will take another little fish for the beautiful cat,' said the fish man, leaning over Tulan in passionate admiration and slapping a whiting as large as a dogfish onto Mrs Miller's enamel dish, 'and on Friday I will be seeing the cat again. There is something to look forward to, Mrs Miller,' he said, standing with his elbow on the gate, watching both of them go up the path, Mrs Miller scrunching and scuffing in her broken slippers and Tulan prancing behind howling and flipping up her back legs. Both he and Mrs Miller, with one mind, had

forgotten the two herrings that Mrs Miller had come out to buy for her dinner.

Having accepted Tulan, Mrs Miller found that it meant what might almost be called hard work. Tulan's passion was inevitably for the front line. She could not be forgotten for hours at a time and satisfied with a stroke and a plate of fish; she would be talked to incessantly, and carried her side of the conversation with a positive conviction; she would not be left alone. Mrs Miller found herself playing exacting games on the stairs, playing bending three feet from the ground to be patted on both temples, playing with balls of paper for Tulan to fly somersaulting round the room without touching the floor. Soon, since Tulan howled when she was left, Mrs Miller began to take her out shopping in the village, held in a fold of her coat. The village people, disapproving, called her 'Mrs Miller's monkey'. Now Tulan slept in bed with her head against Mrs Miller's neck on the pillow, and Mrs Miller put on extra face cream for Tulan to lick off. She was an unsentimental affectionate slut of a creature and Tulan's company suited her down to the ground; the next best thing she was to the right man, and even then less trouble.

Longer and longer the fish man stayed leaning over the gate on Tuesdays and Fridays, talking to both of them; his gifts to Tulan inflated so in size that indeed Mrs Miller would not have been surprised to see him drag a shark out of his van any moment. 'I am thinking I will have to have a cat like this for myself, Mrs Miller,' he said, 'for seeing her twice a week is not enough.' Mrs Miller leaned her elbow on the rotting gatepost and looked over his head. 'What would your wife

think of that?' she said, and the fish man watched Tulan
with a whiting as big as herself and said, 'There is no wife
in my house and never has been.' 'Then who looks after
you?' said Mrs Miller, and he said, 'Why, for sure, I look
after myself. There is no worry for me in not having things as
they should be,' he said, 'for a cat or two and plenty to eat and
a good fire is enough.' 'That's right indeed,' said Mrs Miller,
stooping to run her finger between Tulan's ears. She looked
up at him with her greasy hair falling in her eyes and smirked
to show her white teeth. 'Enough for anyone, for sure,' she
said.

The snow melted and Tulan grew a shade larger and sometimes the fish man stayed talking for an hour or more; when
Tulan was too full of fish to howl for more she would sit on his
shoulder and wash her oriental face, and Mrs Miller would
prop herself against the still rotting gatepost which creaked
on and off under her considerable weight, and they would talk
cats till their throats were dry. This was something for the
village to gossip about under its breath in the shops, how long
the green van stayed outside the cottage; but never more than
a yard from it went Mrs Miller and the fish man, so there was
no surmise of absence to add interest, and for her part Mrs
Miller was secure in herself and cared not a straw what was
said. Now when she looked up over the fish man's head at the
tall line of trees on the hill they were dark with the red colour
of advancing spring. 'This sort of weather I would like to be
going on holiday,' she said to the fish man; and the fish man
said quickly, as if he had been waiting, 'Would you like a little
drive in the van, now?'

Mrs Miller went on staring at the trees in silence; at last she said, 'Indeed that would be a nice change; where is it you will be going from here?' 'Pleased I would be to take you anywhere you want,' said the fish man, 'but if you would like it we could take Tulan to see my cats. Not a very good house, mine is, but she would be welcome.' 'That would be a change for Tulan too,' said Mrs Miller, looking at him carefully and seeming pleased with what she saw. She went flapping up the damp path into the kitchen, and put on her coat, and took eighteen and ninepence out of the teapot on the shelf and her Post Office Savings book from the chaos behind the mangle, and snapped them into a dirty handbag, and went out and shut the door behind her. The fish man leaned on the gate, and Tulan sat on his shoulder beginning to howl for more whiting, for the first lot was an hour past and she had room again. 'She will not have been in a motor before, I expect,' said the fish man, and swung her down on to his arm. 'Well, there is everything ready, then?' he said, looking at Mrs Miller; and Mrs Miller said, 'For sure everything is ready, now,' and shut the gate with a bang that broke the post. Mrs Miller knew, and the fish man knew, that she would not come back to the cottage again except to settle her affairs; but they said nothing.

'There is a fine place for the beautiful cat,' said the fish man, and he put the speechless Tulan into the back of the van with all the sprats and whiting and herrings, and shut the doors.

'A fine place indeed,' said Mrs Miller; and sitting beside him in the front, on a torn fishy cushion, she watched Tulan through the little window while they drove past the Seven Stars and out of the village.

THE ENGLISH LESSON

When Miss Maurer remembered she had to take IVa for English at three, there was no more pleasure in looking out of the staffroom window at the bare trees etched on a winter sky. She turned away towards the fire and her hands were already cold with apprehension. I've got to be firm with them she said in silence, I've got to be, it's not too late to start. She watched how, over a book, the science mistress bent half-smiling, fresh from IVa's biology lesson with not a hair out of place, not a hair stirred by a breath or a movement from the class. Miss Maurer thought in desolation, if I smile they get worse than ever, and if I am stern they laugh behind the desks. A bell rang, and with her stiff, cold fingers she picked up her books and went into the icy corridor that led to the classroom.

All the seventeen children in IVa were sitting on desks and window-sills and arguing passionately about cakes; it was Prue Leigh's birthday and her mother was taking her out to tea. They said, 'Oh, Prue, you don't want to go to Lostriffs'; Lostriffs' are awful.' 'They don't have any with chocolate on.' 'The Bay Tree have jam puffs with sticky on top. Gosh, they're absolutely —' 'Oh, Anna, those are *foul*.' 'Helen, they're *not* foul.' Miss Maurer heard it from the passage. 'Shut up, she's coming.' 'Oh, Lord, *English*.' '*Shelley*.' Touching the frozen brass of the handle, the lunatic desire came to her again, to walk away down the corridor and down the stairs and out of the iron gates at the end of the path and along and away and on down the road. She held the knob for a second, and turned it, and went in.

Every time Miss Maurer faced IVa it seemed to her not possible that they should be no more than seventeen; in dozens, in scores she saw the pure immature lines of their faces turned towards her, their eyes clear or the deceiving light on glasses, scorn and amusement in their mouths and noses, hair impertinently curling or limp with approaching boredom. She touched the desk with her frozen fingers and set her books side by side on the slope. Beyond the window the hills were lighter with snow than the iron sky with the promise of it, and lighter than this malicious dusk in which thirty-four hands shuffled at notes and pencils and Things behind the lids of desks. 'Please,' she said, 'please be quiet at once.' Something in Prue's corner made a noise like a saw; but who would bring a saw to a lesson on Shelley?

Prue said, 'Oh, please, Miss Maurer, I can't see to read.'

'Turn the light on, Mary; I said *Mary*. Helen and Susan, go and sit down.'

'Oh, Miss Maurer, it's awful with the light on.'

'Oh, shut up, it isn't.'

'Shelley,' said someone very low, 'gives me a pain in the . . .'

'Anna, you are *awful*.'

'Neck.'

'Oh, Anna, you *weren't* going to —'

'Page eighteen,' said Miss Maurer; she felt her brows contract, her mouth stretch in a helpless disciplinary mask. 'Mary,' she said. In a quite flat and expressionless voice, as if it were a seed catalogue, Mary began to read.

'O wild west wind thou breath of autumn's being thou
from whose unseen presence the leaves dead are driven
. . .'

Almost before the bell had stopped ringing, Miss Maurer passed the child who held open the door; the child contrived, simply by standing on one leg and sliding a sideways glance, to convey both insolence and relief. Once in the corridor, her fingers warmed and unflexed on the books, she walked with elegance; from one hand she swung a small saw. That was over and she looked forward to Blake with the Sixth, whose hands lay quiet on their desks and who had a good maturing respect for their own language; and then, she thought, I will go out to tea by myself for once, somewhere rich and warm.

Prue went to meet her mother by the Abbey gates, running across the already darkening square in the importance of her birthday, hair curling out and speckled with snow under the round, dark-blue hat. Against the icy flakes in the wind her mother was only two oval dark eyes between the fur of her cap and the fur of her jacket; in fur-lined boots, her feet stamped an expensive pattern on the stones. Like a Czarist lady, she smelt of cold and Cuir de Russie.

When they opened the door of the teashop the warmth, the rosy light, the rich smell of cakes struck almost solid on their faces, almost pressed them back into the street. They sat on gilt chairs against the sweep of petunia curtains shutting out the snow. Prue said, 'I'd like to *live* in a place like this.' 'Vulgar, darling, but at least warm,' said her mother, shedding gloves and furs with the graceful assurance Prue admired but never managed to copy. 'I wish I had a fur coat,' she said. 'A white one.' She looked sideways at the cakes on the tables round them. 'Mary said they didn't have chocolate ones here, and look, it's crawling with them.' 'Chocolate what?' said her mother. 'Darling, did you have a nice day at school?'

'Lousyish,' said Prue; 'well, I mean it was all right. English was quite fun.'

'What did you do in English?'

'Oh, I forget; some sort of poetry, Shelley, I think. I meant we were ragging Maurer.'

'Dearest, I do get them so mixed up; which is Maurer?'

'Oh, Mamma, I've told you; the new one. She's one of those hags – well, she's quite kind and all that, I suppose, but people simply shouldn't *let* themselves, should they? I wouldn't, would you?'

'Let themselves what?' said her mother vaguely.

'Be ragged around with. I mean, if they didn't show it, nobody would, would they? Mamma, you aren't listening.'

'Darling, I'm sorry; I was staring rudely at someone very beautiful and it took my mind off. Do say it again.'

'Oh, where? Mamma, let me see,' said Prue, turning inelegantly.

'The girl over near the door, but you don't have to go into contortions; do sit down.' Prue half-rose from her chair, the cups rocked; she peered over and around the intervening heads. 'Oh, Lord, Mamma, there *is* Maurer; how awful. She couldn't hear what I said from there, could she? She does look pretty cheesed off. What on earth do you think she's doing here? Mamma, I can't see anyone beautiful near the door.'

'Well, never mind; which is Maurer?'

'Well, that one – the hag by herself next to the pillar, with no hat.'

'Darling, that's the one I mean. In a black coat.'

With the overdone surprise so irritating in the very young, Prue sat down and stared speechless at her mother. 'Mamma,' she said at last, 'you *must* be dotty, you must have made a mistake. You can't possibly mean Maurer. I mean, I told you, she's quite awful. It couldn't —'

'You can't be expected to have any taste at your age,' said her mother maddeningly. 'I suppose you think anyone is plain who hasn't got golden curls. I suppose I did too. Maurer is very beautiful indeed, and you'll have to take my word for it.'

'But, oh gosh, what's she *got*? I mean, anyone can see she's a hag; her hair's straight.'

'I know one does at your age, but do you really think people with straight hair are plain just like that?'

'Well, I mean I've got eyes; and, Mamma, she's so *dull*. What on earth *can* you see in her?'

'Choose your cake and let's stop arguing, it's no use at all. Darling, what a pity – you may never see a face like that

again; by the time you're old enough to appreciate it, she'll be teaching some other horrid children, or having broods of her own, and getting wrinkles, not that in her case it would matter a great deal. Do you want the chocolate or the jam?'

'Both, please,' said Prue almost absently. 'Couldn't you ask them to get us some more, Mamma?' she said. 'I still think you're dotty.' Tilting back her chair to an angle from which she could see Miss Maurer's profile colourless in pale and dark against the gilt and petunia wall, she ate steadily through the cakes.

Miss Maurer's tea took her mind off IVa at the time, but in the cold morning she was no more inclined to teach them English grammar than she had been to face them with Shelley the day before; when she sat in the staffroom window at break she could, indeed, hardly bear the thought. Snow had fallen through the night and the glass framed in white feathers the dark trees with white plumes, the hills like swans. She could have watched them unmoving all the morning. But the bell rang; and walking up the corridor she felt the mask of horrid and impotent authority impose itself already on her face. Like ice and lead the books and her fingers froze together.

Prue was sitting on the window-sill above the class; she was saying, 'Well, I know it's rot. It's only what my mother thinks. I mean, she does know about that sort of thing so she ought to know what she's talking about, but she must have had a sort of fit or something. No, but I mean, if she was so absolutely ravishing we could all *see*, or couldn't we?' IVa were enchanted with sensation, united against Prue's mother, yet pleasingly

racked with doubt; they said, 'Oh, Prue, her hair's *straight*; Prue, there must have been something funny about the light; well, your mother must have been looking at someone else; well, we can't all be off our rockers; I mean, she looks like nothing on earth; Prue, are you *sure* it was . . .'

From the corridor, Miss Maurer heard the murmur, the scuffle, the 'Shut up, she's coming'; feebled with apprehension, her fingers burning with cold stuck to the handle, but she went in to a profound silence. Thirty-four eyes were frozen on her face, and Miss Maurer was quite terrified. Oh, heaven, she thought, oh, what are they going to do today? But in this awful vacuum of calm they sat quiet at their desks, not whispering, not scraping, not sawing, only fixing their eyes on her, staring, gazing, as intent as owls. Too unnerved to have more than the dimmest notion of what she was saying, Miss Maurer began at random on the subjunctive mood, but her mind was quite taken up with what in heaven's name they could be staring at. Nothing odd about her clothes, which were the same as yesterday; her skirt was fastened, her suspenders held, both her shoes were black; and, in any case, the eyes all focused on her face. She ran fingers over her hair; it fell on her neck in some disorder of darkness, but not more than usual. It can only be, Miss Maurer said to herself, a very large smut or a smear; but if it is that, why don't they laugh? She turned away from the temptation to leave them and go and look in the staffroom mirror. She went on talking about the subjunctive mood and they went on staring in silence.

The lesson dragged itself in tedium round the clock; but towards its end there was a gradual stirring among the class,

as though it had slept and was slowly wakening. Miss Maurer, in her shell of fear and apprehension, watched it with the beginning of relief. When her questions were answered with a touch of impertinence, when Prue leaned from her desk and whispered to Helen, when heads turned inattentively to look out of the window, she was almost happy; at the first sign of insolence, she smiled. Oh, they're unbearable, Miss Maurer said to herself, but now they are back to normal I nearly like them; anything, anything rather than that shattering stare. And still smiling she looked over their heads to the first patches of green on the white hills, the first melting of the snow.

'Oh, Prue,' said IVa after the lesson, 'do you think your mother was pulling your leg? Oh, Prue, you *don't*!' 'Well, I can see what she means, too.' 'Gosh, Susan, well, you must be cracked.' 'Helen, I'm *not* cracked.' 'Well, you must say, Anna, when she smiled —' 'But I mean, her hair's . . .'

Miss Maurer stood in front of the staffroom mirror, still holding her books in both hands; without expression, her face looked back at her, nothing about it was different. Her eyes, her pallor, the disorder of her hair were those she saw every morning and night, disinterested, in her glass; only her eyes remembered the staring, her mouth the relief of its relaxation; and lifting her shoulders, shaking her head in the conviction she would never know, she moved across to the window and stood looking out at the trees and hills darkening and melting with the thaw.

MISS KING

In the shadow of the stone arch beside the village shop Mrs Young was putting up a polite pretence of being occupied with her order list. Even to herself she would not admit she was lurking. Her hand, sheathed in a perfect pale glove, clasped the warm but unnaturally clean fingers of her child; with the list in her other hand she gestured to bring her platinum watch into view. Lunch was going to be late if Miss King spent more than another five minutes in the shop.

The reason why Miss King in buying her quarter of margarine and two ounces of tea and a candle was causing Mrs Young to lurk undignified under the arch, thus edging her lunch from its ordained time at one o'clock, was not because Miss King was a typhoid carrier, or because she had maligned Mrs Young by telling the village she had murdered her late husband, or because she had a class-conscious feeling about seeing Mrs Young's head rolling in the gutter. Nor was she lousy, or garrulous, or inclined to breathe in anyone's face; none of these things. Mrs Young was hovering out of sight simply because if she went into the shop while Miss King was still there Miss King would give her child a penny.

Lin stood in silence holding her mother's hand. She was thinking out one of her imaginary pieces about a house in a tree. She rubbed her finger against a russet lichen on the wall; the large round grey eyes of her body saw its embroidery on the stone, the larger eyes of her mind watched her own hands hammering split timbers across the branches for a floor. 'Don't do that, darling,' said her mother; 'you'll get so dirty.' Like a machine that shuts itself off automatically, Lin stopped doing it. She could not have repeated what her mother said; the hands were strong and grimed that she saw in her mind's eye nailing planks. Miss King came out of the shop and down the three worn steps as thin as three slices of lemon.

Mrs Young heard the bell twang the all-clear over the shop door; but her powers of self-deception made her take out a little pencil and write Anchovy Essence at the bottom of her list with real enthusiasm. This done, she emerged with an air of purpose from the stone arch into the street and saw Miss King's black-beetle outline diminishing past the cottages towards her hovel, where heaven knew what impoverished meal of bread or powdered milk awaited her. Seething in a well-bred fashion with varied emotions Mrs Young steered Lin into the shop. When they came out the street was deserted; the squat stone houses, the treeless grey and copper arcs of moorland, were remote and self-consciously picturesque as a film set. Mrs Young's emotions receded a little into the intersecting muddled labyrinth of lairs where they crouched when not in use, always at the entrances, always ready to spring. Still holding Lin by the hand she began to walk home.

Miss Emma Bury met them on the corner by the bridge. Two of Emma's horrible little dogs capered round her square shoes; she carried a can of paraffin which slopped on her Harris tweeds every time one of the dogs collided with it, which happened every ten yards or so. Just as some trees are more shapely bare, some buildings more elegant in ruins, so Emma, who at seventeen had been a strapping girl, at fifty-seven was lovely. Mrs Young could, and frequently did, give her a quarter of a century; but time which was going to inflate her flesh on her bones had stripped Emma's down to their shape, and in the long run the stripped win hands down. Mrs Young was vaguely aware of it; her youth was sometimes a cold comfort. But though Emma had about as much finesse as a steamroller Mrs Young was quite fond of her. In the compression of village society it was a question either of liking Emma or of spending six evenings a week with a good book. Mrs Young however thought she liked Emma because Emma was pleasant and not because they were on a sort of social desert island. Emma for her part did not really like Milly Young at all, but she enjoyed her entire stupidity. Mrs Young did not know the difference anyway.

'Good morning, Emma,' she said at the bridge. 'You're ruining your skirt. Are you going home our way? You don't mind if we walk rather quickly, do you?'

'How late you are,' said Emma, not minding but not increasing her pace either. 'Quite ten minutes,' she added with a touch of sarcasm.

'It's *so* slow in the shop.'

'Miss King was slow. We had to hide till she came out,' said the child Lin. Her calculating stare at her mother proclaimed intention rather than the *enfant terrible*. She knew the pattern; already she was moving ahead up the lane before her mother said, 'Darling, run on and tell Phyllis I'm on the way.' Looking distantly up at the vicarage cedar, Mrs Young frowned.

'Of course you know, Milly,' said Emma, 'she baits you on purpose about Miss King.'

'Emma, all children are tactless – in a way it's rather sweet. I don't really think she means it.'

'Rubbish; of course she does. All the village children get given pennies and she has a natural sense of injustice. Didn't you hope someone would give you a penny when you were eight?'

'*Not* a poor old woman who was practically starving.'

'Poppycock, Milly; pure poppycock.'

'Dear Emma, don't let's argue about it again. I've told you, I can't help the way I feel, it's because I'm so stupidly sensitive, I expect. Anyway Lin knows very well she has only to ask me for a penny if she wants one.' Wearing her martyred mother expression, Mrs Young edged unobtrusively behind Emma and reappeared on the side away from the paraffin.

'The point is, she doesn't want a penny or five hundred pounds from you, with your damned maternal duties; a penny from Miss King is a penny from heaven. So help us, we all know its purchasing power is practically nil; but if you could see farther than your conscientious tears, Milly, you'd see that something given you by a stranger from motives of pure

altruism isn't what it appears to be. It's a symbol, you know; even to Lin it's a symbol,' said Emma, becoming warmed up, changing the can to her other hand and wiping the freed one on her skirt.

'Oh, don't be so highbrow, Emma. Do try to see the human side of it – you're so cynical; can't you see how pathetic it is, thinking of that poor old woman with no one belonging to her, living alone on a few shillings a week and giving away pennies she can't afford to all the little children she sees? And not having any of her own, children, I mean. And that awful little hovel and not enough to eat. I simply can't bear to think of Lin taking a penny that might buy bread or milk or something. It's *so* pathetic – can't you *see*?'

'Milly,' said Emma, 'you're a sentimental fool.'

'How *can* you be so hard.'

'Now listen, Milly (not that I haven't told you all this before, God help me); bridge and gardening are your pleasures, and nobody interferes with them. Nobody says it's *so* pathetic how your little hands get soiled with weeds and your little brain moiled with the Vienna Coup. Miss King's pleasure is giving away pennies, and she's got as much right to it as you have to yours. If she doesn't give a penny to Lin she gives it to another child. What Miss King eats is none of your business, Milly; and if you don't stop dodging about behind me I shall pour this blasted paraffin over your new shoes. Think it over,' said Emma, stamping off up the track that led to her house, with her nasty capering dogs and her bland stony face and her hair like steel shavings. In her wake went the draught of Reason, and folded in the reassembling emotional clouds Mrs

Young trailed up the hill towards her lunch, up the small lane that led among rocks, bracken and heather on the bare hillside, to her white house that looked like a villa at Sainte-Maxime, its exotic garden carved out of the desert moor. She dabbed from her sleeve the drops of paraffin and from her eyes the tears of charity; she was thinking it over. Emma couldn't hope to understand. So terribly, terribly heart-rending, said Mrs Young, letting herself in through the wrought-iron gate.

Up came Emma the next afternoon but one for her Thursday tea at the villa. The howls of her furious uninvited little dogs pursued her on the thin wind. Sunlight as austere as the hills stencilled its shadows on the rocks and on her face; she walked in her bracken tweeds as undisclosed and uncompromising as a moving piece of country. Familiarity did not lessen in Emma the amusement of being hit in the eye by Milly's villa on turning a shoulder of rock; set in its cypresses, fandangled *à la Côte d'Azur* with striped sunblinds and fuchsia and geranium on the white terrace, it continued to remind her of one of those surrealist landscapes of Louis Quatorze clocks or lace-edged eyeballs on a large empty beach. Emma could see nevertheless that when one knew Milly it attained a kind of logic; thus Milly in a world of chaos was wrapped in unreality. Knows nothing about Life, said Emma to herself, opening the scrolled gate; nothing whatever.

Milly's child in grey flannel shorts swung her feet over Emma's head from a branch of the cedar tree. Emma was fond of Lin; the world of Lin's imagination, she suspected, was a more ordered place than the world she lived in with her

mother. Looking up into the tree, Emma stood smiling in the slightly greenhousish warmth of Milly's garden, reluctant to progress into the orchid drawing-room heat. Lin folded her arms on the branch and leaned down to peer with the air of one falsely indecisive at the confessional; seeming at last satisfied with Emma's discretion she felt in the pocket of her shorts and held up a penny.

'Nice work, Lin,' said Emma shamelessly. 'Keep it hidden.'

'I've got a box,' said Lin, charmed with conspiracy. 'I've got four in it. With shells on.'

Emma mentally removed the descriptive phrase from the pennies and applied it to their container, without comment. Milly would have said 'Not the pennies, darling; the box.'

'Yesterday I got this one,' said Lin, 'in the afternoon, when I came on in front, when the Vicar was there. It's got a key; I keep it in some paper in my party shoes.'

'Lin Young,' said Emma, who liked the sound of the child's absurdly Chinese name, 'what's so particular about Miss King's pennies?'

Lin considered. Over her head the dark tree spread like thunder on a light sky; secrecy folded them in its shade, she suspended over Emma's head, Emma squared on the dry needles of the path. 'Well – she doesn't know me,' she said at last.

'Quite,' said Emma. She stumped off to look for Milly on the terrace, coming out of the tree's compass as from a cave into the full sun. But the terrace was deserted; reflecting on its silly likeness to a setting for a worldly play, Emma went through the French windows into the drawing-room. Here

Milly sat in her looped and draped fashion on a cyclamen settee. Her nose was pink; with a theatrical handkerchief she dabbed at each eye in turn. Hell, thought Emma. Visions of tea in the sun with her feet up disintegrated; now she was to be cried over in Milly's overpowering salon. Milly's 'Oh, Emma!' broke in the middle. Emma sat down ungracefully and took out a cigarette; she was all thumbs when it came to a scene.

'Emma, it's so awful. I don't know how to tell you.'

'Well, just say it; what is?'

'You'll never understand – you never know how I feel. It's Miss King.'

'Oh is it? Has she given —'

'*Don't*, Emma; she's dead.'

'Oh.'

'You're like a stone,' said Milly, flooding on a rising note.

'Well, I understand all right; why shouldn't I? It's plain enough. Naturally I'm sorry. But after all,' said Emma reasonably, 'she was quite seventy, and it must have been good and quick. That's the way I'd like it. How did you find out?'

'I rang up Trump about the f-fish; they'd only – he'd only just heard. It happened about an hour ago, quite s-s-suddenly. Emma, isn't it pathetic . . .?'

'No more pennies,' said Emma tactlessly, after a pause.

Milly overflowed. 'Emma, how *can* you be so —'

'Listen, Milly,' said Emma, 'you'd better get over it alone. I don't seem to have the right reactions. Ring me up if you want me to come to tea tomorrow. Now don't let's argue.' She disregarded Milly's drenched social protests; haloed in an exasperated cloud of smoke, her fingers itching with the need to shake Milly, she made her way along the terrace, down the flagged path to the cedar's shade. Under the tree she stopped and looked up at Lin on the branch. Better straight from a plain woman than wrapped up from a foolish one, she thought to herself. Besides that, she wanted to see how Lin would take it. Emma knew her own true motives.

'Aren't you coming to tea?' said Lin from over her head.

'Lin,' said Emma, stamping her cigarette into the path, 'did you know Miss King was dead?' She watched the child's face against the dark tree.

'Oh no,' said Lin, 'she isn't. She gave me one.'

'That was yesterday. She died this afternoon.'

'Won't she give me any more?'

'Well, she can't, can she?'

'Well, she might want to.'

'Even if she wants to, she can't now. I expect she would if she could. She liked doing it.'

'Poor Miss King,' said Lin. 'I wanted to get six. I wanted her to give me another.'

'Hard luck,' said Emma ambiguously, opening the gate. She went home and let out her little dogs, whistling them to follow her on the road to the village. As she walked, hoping vaguely that someone would invite her to tea, she frowned at the cold rock and drying bracken of the moor. Her dogs capered, and the wind that had left Milly's garden in an island of calm lifted her iron curls on her forehead. Miss King, thought Emma, crossing the bridge, would have preferred Lin's epitaph to Milly's. Such a nerve Milly has, she said to herself, such a nerve, ascribing pathos uninvited. She'll leave all her money to a cats' home; the poor, poor pussies, she'll say, it's *so* pathetic; and half Europe starving. The village was deserted again, the children not yet out of school. Only one small boy, the youngest Bullen child, stood in nervous anticipation staring in the crowded window of the shop, sideways up the street, back to the tins and tapes and sweets behind the glass. Emma's square shadow fell; he looked at her absently.

'Why aren't you in school?' said Emma. Violent personal questions were the small change of her conversation; she would have said to a duke in the same tone, 'Why aren't you in the House of Lords?' Either you were insulted or you took it in the intended spirit; Emma neither knew nor cared which.

'They'm singen,' said the child, such interrogation being familiar.

'Don't you sing?'

'Carn't.'

Without pursuing the subject, which smelt a thought fishy, Emma said, 'What have you got in your hand?'

'Thrippence.' Tom disclosed three pennies on a rank palm. Straight downward lashes striped his light eyes with black; straight hair at the same angle striped his forehead. He looked past Emma up the street.

'What are you going to buy?'

'That gun,' said the child, pointing his finger at a cardboard cannon.

'Well, why don't you buy it?'

'He'm fourpence.'

'Oh-ho,' said Emma, seeing the suspected light, 'you think you're going to get the rest from Miss King. Well, you won't. She won't give you any more pennies. She's dead.'

Tom stopped looking past Emma; his striped eyes fixed on her with an air of baffled anguish. Emma was not proof against it. Almost automatically her hand felt in one pocket for a penny and she held it out towards Tom. They stared at each other.

'Go and buy the gun,' said Emma irritably. 'What are you waiting for?'

Tom took the penny, with a child's unselfconscious animal gesture. He was no longer anguished; in his stare, along with surprise and renewed hope, Emma saw a touch of calculation. While she stood on the pavement and heard the bell announce his entrance, more distant, as if in echo, the school bell rang. Indecisive, for once at a loss, Emma went on standing. Finally it seemed her mind was made up; instead of frowning she smiled with malice, thinking of Milly.

'Miss King is dead; long live Miss King,' she said out aloud; and taking half a crown out of her pocket she crossed the street towards the Post Office, to exchange it for thirty pennies.

THE RIVER

From north to south the river flowed straight through the town, but in so strange a way that no one who walked or drove in the streets could have told there was a river there at all. As rivers go, it was a very minor affair, and those people who called the town a village called it a stream; but these were mostly visitors. Besides its hidden and furtive course, there was another oddity about the river, which was that it had two names; but as neither was ever used by the local inhabitants, that was of no consequence except to map-readers. In itself, the river only attained importance as somewhere to throw things, and as a place to keep ducks, and as a menace after much rain, and finally, as a great affair of interest in the lives of two people. These were William and his daughter, Frankie; and between their ages there was a difference of just fifty years.

William was a Londoner who had grown tired of London suddenly, eight years ago. Eight years ago, with a suitcase and his savings, he had taken a third-class single ticket to a small town in Devon with a romantic name, a name, at least, that seemed romantic to him, and there bought a shop. The risks

and obstacles attendant on such madness merely disintegrated at the impact of a character which, to be thus mad, was clearly out of the ordinary. The grocery shop flourished. Four years later, William married a local girl in whom he saw qualities as unusual as his own. Emmy was not quite half his age. After eighteen months, Frankie was born; and at nearly fifty-three, William found himself united with his child of two and a half over their common passion, the river.

Though Emmy shared most of William's interests, about this one she was no more than nicely tolerant; the pleasure she took in the river was the indirect one of its providing William and Frankie with something to do on early-closing days, thus leaving her free to go and visit her mother and sit in the warm kitchen or the fresh, untidy garden of the farm, drinking cups of strong tea and not talking. Emmy did not like any of the things that amuse most young women; that was one of the reasons William had married her. She disliked knitting, and gossiping, and jazz, and making blouses out of curtain-lace, and looking in shop windows; she disliked buying clothes, and wore the ones she did buy long after most women would have tired of them, and replaced them by going very quickly into a shop and buying something else almost exactly the same. She made Frankie's clothes in what she called her working hours; and in the evenings she sat and read books about famous murder trials and Polar exploration, and listened to records of the music of Sibelius.

When the shop closed on Wednesdays, and Emmy had gone off to her mother's, William and Frankie would set out, bent on the enjoyment of their unvarying routine. To begin

with, they would walk right up the main street to the end of the town, which, at Frankie's pace, took them at least ten minutes. All the morning, set going after breakfast by William, Frankie would have been saying like a little machine, 'See ve river; see ve river'; but as soon as they left the house through the green door with a brass lion's-head knocker, next to the shop, they behaved as if they were out with no more object than a stroll in the country. And when they reached the last houses, and the twenty yards of railings and a little bridge, which was the only place in the whole town where the stream was to be seen from a road, they would both shout in a chorus of bogus surprise, '*There's* the river!' For five or ten minutes, leaning in identical attitudes with their elbows on the white railings, William on the top bar and Frankie on the lowest, they would stare at the narrow, clear water rushing over bluish stones below their feet, and parting from the road to dive behind the houses and out of sight. Then, hand in hand, they would walk back down the street to the next place.

There, between two shops, a little dark stone tunnel with a pointed arch cut right through a house, and you walked over the unseen river and came out on an unsuspected and quite ravishing deserted scene that looked like somewhere abroad. One side of the water was a grassy path wavering past cottages, the other rose straight into the uneven, insecure backs of the houses on the main street; and between them the river flowed and vanished under the shallow arch of a house built clean on top of it. In the blue shadow of this arch, all the ducks gathered, and by bending down you saw them floating

quietly between the water and the ripples of light cast up on the stone. From this viewpoint, to be truthful, there was no building in sight that was not a slum; here William had to stifle a conscience that pricked him with thoughts of damp and rheumatism and social responsibility. But his pleasure in the scene was only a little lessened. As for Frankie, she neither knew nor cared.

When they had finished looking, and Frankie had spent some time bending down with her head against her knees and her behind stuck in the air like one of the ducks she peered at, they would go back through the tunnel to the street and in twenty yards turn off again up a narrow lane; here a humped bridge spanned the river, and beside it was a little space paved with large pieces of slate, and a minute weir, and a view of the water flowing on in a narrow cleft between the high, uneven, ferny stone walls of the houses on either side. The house by the bridge was built out on stone pillars over the stream, and sometimes the ducks would come drifting through, under it and into the light. On occasions, someone would have tied a piece of dried and salted cod to the spikes in the weir with a length of string, hoping by this carefree and insanitary method to keep the smell of its soaking out of the house. William and Frankie always liked to see these pieces of cod, and William always wondered, but never found out, whether they were forgotten or washed away or salvaged by a water-minded cat, or whether they really did get eaten in the end. He also wondered why all the houses had back doors with steps leading down into the river; but though he kept asking people, no one ever seemed to know.

The lane and the stream parted company; the lane emerged into the street that crossed the main street, and the river flowed underneath it. By trespassing into the yard of the mill on the other side and opening a door between the granary and a pile of coal, William and Frankie got in another view; but after that they had to go a long way round, up to the church and back by a footpath round the churchyard's edge, before they came to the river again at the point they both liked best. William liked it because it was so tranquil and rustic, because the grey tower and gilded clock of the ancient church rose against hills and above yew trees, and the river came confined between the thick grey walls of gardens and ran under a round bridge and then down the edge of a field; and Frankie liked it because two steps by the bridge led down to the water, and because of the shoe and the marrow.

The shoe was someone's discarded black one, beached on a small strip of sand at the bottom of the wall, and it had been there all the summer, since the spring rains. Later the marrow had joined it a yard or so away, caught in a dead bush just above the stream. It was clearly an uneatable marrow, for a rat had started on one end and gone away discouraged; but it was very smooth and bright yellow, and appealed enormously to Frankie, who behaved as if each time she saw it was the first, saying, 'Look, Daddy; a MARROW in ve river! A SHOE in ve river; Daddy, *look*!'

William would sit on the wide parapet of the bridge, lighting his pipe and watching Frankie jump and shout on the lower step. He did not say 'Be careful', or 'Don't get your feet

wet', or 'Mind you don't fall in', any more than Emmy ever said 'Don't fall off the table' or 'Mind how you come down the stairs', because they both thought that children have more sense than they are credited with, and that nobody falls anywhere on purpose, so that warnings are rather a waste of breath. Except for being trained to look before crossing the road, Frankie was left alone to learn by experience, and as yet had neither fallen down the stairs or in the river nor set herself alight. William, therefore, could sit quite peacefully on the bridge and look at his child, taking a sober pleasure in her beauty; for both he and Emmy were pleasantly but irrevocably plain.

From the moment when they left the shoe and the marrow, and went, with Frankie talking about them incessantly, up another footpath round the churchyard, they also left the town; but there was one more bridge to visit, where the river curved round through a marshy field, and you could stand and see all the hills that enclosed the town, rising high to the north, and to the south more gently rounded. Here the landmarks were of the country, and William and Frankie had seen at different times a trout lying still in the shadow, a heron, a kingfisher, and once when the river was very low, two geese hiking pathetically in single file, ankle-deep, with the plodding yet flurried air of someone who has to get some-where before dark and can't get a lift.

From this bridge they walked home through narrow lanes to the shop, and William would give Frankie her tea while they waited for Emmy to return in time to bath her; and Frankie, half asleep after walking well over a mile, would go to bed

smiling and muttering about the river, the marrow, and the shoe.

All through the winter, before Frankie's third birthday, she and William did their tour of the river on Wednesday and Sunday afternoons. The weather was mostly dry and cold, and Frankie wore slate-blue trousers like a ski-suit and a dark-red hood and gloves, and William wore an overcoat which he had bought in London nine years ago, and which Emmy, unlike most wives, did not pester him to discard. In the dark arch of the house over the river the ducks were hardly to be seen; the shoe became more bloated, the marrow more shrivelled, but to William's relief neither was carried away, for Frankie's affection towards them seemed rather to increase than to lessen with time.

Then early in the year it began to rain. It rained with a warm, insistent flood that showed no signs of stopping. On the first Sunday it rained so hard that even William and Frankie had to stay at home and Emmy had to come back from the farm in her mother's gumboots because the lane was four inches deep in mud and water. William thought gloomily about the fate of the shoe and the marrow. On the Tuesday morning, when it had rained all night, he looked out of the shop door down the gentle slope of the street (for the shop was not in the main street but in the one leading up to the church) and saw a dozen people frantically sweeping the river out of the Star Hotel, the White Lion and the bank on the corner, and the river implacably flowing not under but across the street and in at the doors again. William left Emmy to deal with the shop, and went down with a broom to help.

All the time he was sweeping water and making suggestions about seeing if the drains were clear (they weren't but no one had thought of it) he held in his mind's eye a dismal little picture of Frankie's shoe and marrow bobbing on the flood of the distant estuary towards the raging sea. About midday the water went down an inch or two, the drains were cleared of dead leaves, and to the disappointment of some Jonahs the crisis seemed to be over.

In some apprehension, William walked Frankie up the main street the next afternoon, hoping the volume of water would distract his daughter's mind from what it had destroyed; and indeed, the little river, so sternly kept out of sight, had at last attained a magnificent and revengeful importance. The grassy path had gone, and thus widened, and no longer clear but an angry reddish-brown, it came roaring between the whitewashed slums and into the shallow arch, where the wall of the house rose from a curling wing of foam. Frankie was enthralled. Since she expressed no anxiety about the ducks, William grew more optimistic concerning the shoe and the marrow. They made their way over the humped bridge, but the slate-paved yard was under water and a barrier of wood fixed in two ancient slots kept it from washing into the lane. Finally, they went round the churchyard walk and came to their favourite place, which was now a fine sight with the steps submerged, a howling torrent an inch below the path. William looked anxiously at Frankie, and Frankie anxiously at the river; at the moment when William said hurriedly, 'Cor, *look* at all the water', Frankie began to roar. William could find nothing strange or spectacular enough to distract her

anguish; abandoning the idea of struggling on to the last bridge, he led her, bawling 'See ve MARROW! See ve SHOE!', back under the dripping trees, along the wet path and home to the shop.

In time, Frankie's tears dried up, but her interest and confidence in the river had been bitterly shaken; William could no longer take her to the bridge near the church without suffering a minor repetition of the same scene. He was amazed at the maddening and unflagging memory of childhood, and began to wonder if shoes and marrows had some deep psychological significance. This he suggested to Emmy, who gave her slow smile and said nothing. But William was a creature of determination; and when the waters subsided, as they did in a few days, in inflexible and purposeful silence he set about finding another shoe and another marrow.

It seemed to him that in the past he had rarely walked anywhere without seeing one of those aged, discarded shoes that lie around in ditches and gutters, and that one passes without a second glance or more than a fleeting wonder about who put them there and why; but now that he wanted one, it was only to be expected that there was none to be found. He went so far as to ask Emmy if she had any worn-out shoes she could give him, and Emmy said no; but she did not ask him what he wanted them for, which was another of the reasons William had married her. William took to bolting his lunch and dashing out in the midday closing hour on a bicycle, since it was dusk when the shop shut and there was never time before it opened; and finally one day he came back with something stuffed into the saddle-bag and dripping through

the corners, and in silent triumph took it upstairs and hid it in the wardrobe.

After that, the whole battery of William's purpose became focused on the marrow. He had a small garden behind the shop, but there were no vegetables in it, and it went without saying that marrows were out of season. However, they could at least be stored; and William, thanking heaven that Frankie's subconscious fancies had not picked on a nectarine or a horse-mushroom, set himself in clumsy and amateurish diplomacy to draw the conversation with his friends and acquaintances round to the subject of keeping vegetables for the winter. Unfortunately, all William's friends were deeply bitten with the gardening bug, and when William suggested that marrows, after long storing, became woody and were no use, they were all affronted, and said some people's marrows might, but not theirs. Eventually, after spending quite a lot of time and money on half-pints of bitter and cider, William met a farm labourer called Viner who was honest or disinterested enough to admit that even the rats wouldn't eat half the marrows he had stored in his cottage attic.

William, rushing back from the bar with two pints of rough, said, blushing faintly, that he had a notion to make something for his child out of a useless marrow; a smallish one, said William, about *so* long, and a nice bright yellow. And the next evening he met Viner in the same bar, and Viner gave him a smallish yellow marrow that felt like a piece of mahogany, and William bought two more pints of rough. They stayed talking for a time, Viner in his soft, broad Devon dialect and William in a voice in which the same soft

vowels were supplanting the sharp tones of a London accent; and then William took the marrow home and put it in his wardrobe with the shoe.

On the following Tuesday evening it was clear and fine, the stars bright. Emmy's character (which had got her where she was now, sitting under a 60-watt electric bulb, reading about Eskimos and listening to Sibelius's Second, instead of delivering calves in a messy shed or doing things with egg accounts under an oil lamp, so perhaps it deserved this reward) allowed her to watch William go through the sitting-room and out into a dry night, wearing gumboots and carrying a shoe and a paper parcel, and not say a word. Amiably disinterested, she went back to the Eskimos; her mind simply glanced off William's eccentricities. William, with a hollow, rubbery sound, clumped round the frosty path by the churchyard to the bridge and the steps; stopping to look for observers, clutching the marrow to his breast with an unconsciously melodramatic air, he plunged into the icy shallow water and laid his trophies, like someone sacrificing at an altar, in their appointed places on the far side of the stream.

Willingly enough, but without great enthusiasm, Frankie walked beside William up the main street early the next afternoon. Her small hand in a clean, dark-red glove held William's in a large, dirty leather one, and William, bursting with pride and anticipation, looked down at her small face clear as a shell in the blue and dark-red hood. It was sunny, and in a touch of frost the running light glittered on the water that was now quick but shallow and transparent as glass. But before they reached the river at the top of the street,

William's desire to see Frankie's pleasure over the marrow and the shoe got the better of his liking for routine; and halfway up he swung her around and they began to walk back, passing the tunnel and the lane and the mill, and going up to the churchyard path. Frankie looked surprised, but acquiesced. Smiling idiotically to himself, William led her past the bleached gravestones, awry under the bare trees, past the thin railings and along to the water lapping under the little bridge; there they stopped on the two steps, and William, dashing a glance across the stream and seeing the shoe and the marrow as convincing as if time had gone back, bent down to watch his child's face.

Frankie looked at the thin, bright river over the bluish stones, at the sunlight on the branches, at the blue shadow under the bridge; and in a sudden and frightful roar she bawled, 'See ve BIG water! See ve BIG water!'

Losing his temper with equal suddenness, William howled above the din, 'Damn and blast, aren't you never satisfied?'

'See ve BIG water!' shrieked his child.

William seized her hand and began to stride away from the river; all the pints of cider, the bicycle rides with gnawing indigestion, the talks about marrows and the splash of icy water in his gumboots rose before his mind's eye; and frowning in an awful silence, he led the bellowing Frankie back along the footpath, under the cold trees and past the tombstones in the direction of the shop.

THE TWO MRS REEDS

Lucy's quick moving, her air of confidence, sat oddly on a new patient; when she came through the swing doors of the ward, on the rebound of Sister's advance, the six women in maternity looked at her with a touch of curiosity. Her manner towards the dragon Sister might almost have been called matey. If they had not already graduated from labour to convalescence the women would have found encouragement in this brisk and competent attitude; as it was, they sensed in her a kind of liaison joining staff and patient. Suspended still between the world and the ward, Lucy was part of neither and of both.

Lucy herself was aware of this division more than they. Her labour had not begun; not yet by circumstance made passive in bed, she refuted the passive role of a walking patient, using her medical knowledge, her familiarity with hospital routine, as a lever to ease herself halfway on to the staff. This was her second child; she knew her way. At the birth of her first two years ago she had made herself remembered less by the difficulties of her confinement than by her passionate clinical interest in its stages. Her questions were not of the kind to be fobbed off with 'Never mind, dear'; she

knew too much; she would be answered. Now this familiarity, this gulf of knowledge, separated her from the ward. Talking to the women while she unpacked into her locker, Lucy sensed the total difference of attitude, which was in part emphasised by Sister's remark as with a plate of green and red pills she flashed past the almost exclusively literary contents of Lucy's suitcase: 'Mrs Furneaux, dear, are you here for a baby or a reading course?' Not only this, but Lucy seemed to treat her pregnancy with irreverence; showing unnatural bravado in the face of nature, she ran up the ward in Sister's absence, climbed on window-sills to adjust the ventilation, and got on her bed with a sort of vault. The women were amused, but a little shocked. It was to them no less eccentric that Lucy should take pleasure in the surroundings, the atmosphere and the smell of hospital, in their eyes a kind prison from which God speed their release. When Lucy, saying she was cheesed off with smocks, had gone to change into a dressing-gown the thought circulated unspoken, She'll tell a different story when she starts; but they only half believed it.

Once in her dark wool gown severely corded round what she hoped would soon be her waist, Lucy felt herself entirely an initiate; her clothes from the world were laid aside. Now she was at last severed from reality, from responsibility quite cut off, bound for a period into the rule and routine of women, as if in a clinical convent. By tea-time she was on terms with everyone; with the nurses, who found her as knowledgeable as an extra nurse; with the patients, whom she amused by her excessive activity. She became no longer part of neither world, but an intimate of both.

By morning the ward had come round to the view that she would have her baby with the same competence. There was no surprise when she breezed into the kitchen at half-past eleven saying her contractions had begun; the word Pains was omitted from Lucy's vocabulary, she said it had the wrong psychological effect. With unabated energy she came back to the ward and brushed her hair, tied it from her face with a black ribbon, went off to the labour room as unconcernedly as to the bath. The women were deeply interested in the progress of Lucy's confinement, exacting bulletins from the nurses. At noon Nurse Field told them Lucy was arguing with Sister that she was having second stage contractions, a theory which was ridiculed by Sister but subsequently proved to be accurate. At half past twelve Lucy had eaten her way through roast mutton, turnips and rice pudding. At one she had told Nurse Howe that it was not painful and all a question of psychology, and at one-fifty, refusing an anaesthetic, she had produced a daughter and argued with Sister about sitting up to look at it. If it had not been for their acquaintance with Lucy, and for the fact that no sounds had indeed issued from the labour room except an occasional buzz of hilarity, the women would have been incredulous; but they could not in any case dispute the panache of her return to the ward, delayed till tea-time by the arrival of visitors at two. By that time one might almost have expected Lucy to walk back; even her bed, propelled by Sister and Nurse Field, seemed to move at a speed unlike the beds of other patients. Lucy was still amiably arguing. Re-established in the corner farthest from the door, provided with a large tea, she began to tell everyone about how she had enjoyed herself. After that she leaned on her elbow and wrote letters very fast. Sister went off duty and the social temperature rose.

Between seven and eight was the visiting hour for husbands; here again circumstance and conditioning separated Lucy from the others. Their men were all in the Forces, some on leave, some abroad; Louis was a farmer. That in itself was barely eccentric; but the man was not only agricultural but French, and not only that but he and Lucy behaved with a facetious disregard of all the conventions of affection; for the hour of his visit they laughed, argued, insulted each other happily in French and English. The other husbands who were on leave almost knelt by their wives' beds. When Louis departed, telling the nurse his baby was a fright, Lucy felt she had become in the eyes of the ward finally inhuman. The affection they felt for her was the affection one gives to a pet monkey. But encircled in knowledge, unbroken by emotion, her relationship with the staff remained normal; she was the best patient.

When the visitors left an air of anti-climax, of boredom, settled on the ward. Books seemed unreadable; babies and bedpans precluded an early retiring for the night. Disinclined to read and now fettered with the realisation that for nine days she was condemned to inactivity as surely as if she were in chains, Lucy watched through the long windows the light dissolving to dusk over the distant harbour. Approaching night was one of the less pleasing moments in hospital; with the drawn curtains, the lights, the conscription of staying in bed and the routine of sleep came a sense almost of

claustrophobia. Before the babies were brought in a new patient arrived; but since she went straight to the labour room the only stir she caused in the ward came indirectly from Lucy, who, when Nurse Field told them Mrs Reed was getting on nicely, said vaguely, 'I used to be called Reed, too.'

'Before you were married?' said Mrs Skilling from the opposite corner.

'My first husband,' said Lucy, dropping another minor bomb; seeing that everyone wondered and no one cared to ask when and where he had been killed, she added, 'I divorced him.'

The other patients looked at her as if she had said, 'I ate him'; Mrs Skilling, recovering neatly, called from her corner, 'Was he a bad lot, dear?'

'He was six kinds of a pig,' said Lucy. Sitting up in bed in a white silk jacket buttoned to the neck, with her black hair tied like a child's and the grey tulips Louis had brought on the locker beside her, she had an air of such expensive innocence that it was difficult to believe either in the birth of her baby eight hours before or in a Past containing a criminal and discarded husband. (All the women concluded Mr Reed had been a monster, had probably and at the least beaten his wife; casual unpleasantness was meant to be suffered, not brought into court.) Fearing lest Lucy had feelings after all – though this hardly now seemed possible – they would not enquire further. Lucy in fact would have been quite happy to tell them about the maddening Thomas Reed, and indeed had opened her mouth to say she hadn't been able to stand being called bohemian every time he opened his, but the babies

postponed her confidence. All the women wanted to see Lucy's daughter; and though Lucy and Louis had agreed that to anyone with an objective view it must be clear how like a little ape she was, they all said 'Bless her, she's lovely.' With this extrovert vision Lucy was aware that almost all the babies, ugly though they might be, were better-looking than hers. She was not dismayed; her first child, Guy, even more simian at birth, had quickly grown into beauty; this baby with the same heritage would change after the same fashion. Nevertheless at present it *was* a fright. Lucy said so; no one believed in her conviction.

About three o'clock in the morning they brought in Mrs Reed; the wheels of her bed squeaked, effectively waking the ward. She came in like any patient except Lucy, quiet in the faint light from the passage, flattened; the line of her body hardly raised shadows in the counterpane. Lucy, irrational in her disturbed sleep, took an instant dislike to her. Through one prejudiced eye she watched Mrs Reed trolleyed into place next to her own bed, hovered over, left in the mystic silence of someone who has gone through it with the wrong psychological approach; her nose is too sharp, she said to herself, and turned over, and slept.

In the morning (not the false dawn of tea and washing, temperatures and babies and bedpans from a quarter to five till six, but that moment when you woke again to the full sun and finding yourself in the middle of the ward with a chair on your feet and the day staff sweeping where your bed had been) Lucy's attitude to Mrs Reed became one of a fainter and more reasoned antipathy. It was difficult to dislike people

whole-heartedly till you had heard them speak. Mrs Reed, though she recovered quickly from being flattened and soon had knees and feet under the counterpane like everyone else, seemed disinclined to open her mouth. Lucy and the other patients proffered the amiable trivialities; 'Yes,' said Mrs Reed, or 'No'; but that was all. Whatever Lucy's moral views might be, her social code was strict; if for no other reason than that life should be as pleasant as possible she believed in the duty of man towards man, that one should shut doors behind one, give up one's seat in the bus, eat silently, and bear one's part in the conversation with as much ease and animation as one could command. People who did none of these things, Lucy considered, were socially about as useful as bed-bugs. Giving her the benefit of her condition, Lucy shut up till Mrs Reed should see fit to make a move; it was now up to her.

In any case, when one talked, one talked to the whole ward; conversations with the next bed had a way of becoming immediately general. When the subject was not confinements it was children, homes or knitting; though she was seldom unwilling to talk, it was not long before Lucy would have enjoyed a change to books or politics; but here there was no common ground. She was not much interested in other people's children; she liked the wrong kind of house and she did not knit. Nevertheless she discussed bed-wetting, three-piece suites and cardigan patterns as if all were familiarities in the Furneaux household; in the intervals she read something heavy, and wished she could be allowed to smoke.

The following afternoon (Mrs Reed being apparently in excellent health but still tacit) Lucy was sitting up in bed

vaguely thinking about her. Spring sunlight flooded the ward through the high windows, lay in pools on the polished amber wood of the floor; Louis's grey tulips stood curling open on the centre table, with white narcissi on either side. Sister was off duty and the nurses laughed in the kitchen. While Lucy's senses were enjoying the sun and the ward, and her hands were occupied in cutting cord dressings from a roll of lint, her mind was busy putting Mrs Reed into a catalogue of types. Mrs Reed's nose was not as sharp as Lucy had at first thought, but her hair was lank and looped into a knot and she had an emotional look in her eye when her baby was brought in, which Lucy mistrusted. She wore a mauve bed-jacket knitted in a shell pattern. Always cleaning the house, Lucy said to herself, lace tablecloths, probably goes to chapel; doesn't swear, doesn't smoke, drink or paint the face; doesn't lose her temper with children; has little weeping scenes in corners hidden away where someone will find her; no, let me not be malicious as well as an intellectual snob, cross that out, but I fear she's a prig all the same. Pleased with her classification, Lucy finished the cord dressings and lay back enjoying the sun, the ward, the absence of household cares, and everything else except the wireless. As soon as Sister went off duty someone asked one of the nurses to switch on. Lucy and Sister were united in a dislike of jazz; as soon as Sister came in she switched it off. For this Lucy felt a positive affection towards her, which in Lucy was a good deal; and everyone else liked her less, which was very little indeed. Now condemned till five o'clock to hear jungle noises or worse, Lucy sighed and abandoned the thought of reading the *New Statesman*; instead

she reached for her dressing-case, combed her hair, tried out a new candy-pink lipstick and voiced again her need for a cigarette.

'There's gasping I am for one too,' said Mrs Reed, as suddenly as if someone had at last wound her up.

Lucy's social code deserted her; she looked for a moment almost stunned. The fact that Mrs Reed had in one sentence clicked out of the catalogue was not the only surprise. 'You're Welsh,' said Lucy accusingly.

'Machynlleth,' said Mrs Reed, sounding like a block in the cistern.

Her grounds for dislike thus doubly cut away from under her feet (for unlike most of the English she loved the Welsh), Lucy had to reconsider Mrs Reed in the light of her nationality and her vices. The picture was quite altered. She was for once glad of the wireless which enfolded them in intimacy; the rising, singing notes of Mrs Reed's accent were a kind of substitute for the music she would have liked to hear. They talked of Wales.

'My first husband was called Reed, too,' said Lucy much later.

'There's coincidence, now,' said Mrs Reed; 'a lucky name it's been for me. Glad I am of the day I met mine, indeed. Was he nice to you?'

'Horrible he was,' said Lucy, who had been trying out a Welsh accent under Mrs Reed's tuition. 'So I divorced him,' she added in her normal voice.

'I would do it myself if it was like that,' said Mrs Reed; 'wasting time it is to stay together when you don't get on.'

'Wouldn't you get cheesed off if your husband kept telling you how to run the house?'

'I would indeed.'

'Not I must say that my housekeeping is very polished,' said Lucy. 'I expect I don't feel about it the way I should; but that's no reason to keep telling me I ought to live in a caravan. Rudeness I can't stand, can you? Anyway there wasn't anything we did agree about, except parting.'

'Very young you were when you married him, isn't it?'

'Nineteen.'

'What can you expect, now? Twenty-eight I was. Old enough to know my own mind, and no better husband than Tom could I hope for.'

'Tom?'

'Thomas his name is; what was yours?'

'Daniel,' said Lucy rather wildly; a sudden irrational and absurd conviction held her. Impossible as it seemed, it was the sort of thing that would happen in any events involving Thomas; and, malice apart, this was their part of the country; it was not unnatural that Thomas should have returned here after they parted in London. Lucy began to stack the pile of dressings, scissors on top, saying with the same uninflected interest, 'What does he look like?'

'Here he is, see,' said Mrs Reed, diving into her locker and throwing across to Lucy a photo of Thomas that almost turned her up. He was wearing a uniform, and saying to the photographer, Man, look at the *dust* on your camera. Lucy murmured something; what it was she never knew. Years of social training came to her rescue, and with a feeling she was going to see the funny side of it at any moment she said, 'What a magnificent piece. Mine was fair.'

'Very dark Tom is. There's a joke it would have been,' said Mrs Reed, laughing, 'if they were the same.'

Lucy gave what the women novelists call a mirthless smile, saying, 'Where's he stationed?' All unselfish thoughts of Mrs Reed's married happiness were discarded; she prayed for Burma.

'Bristol,' said Mrs Reed. 'Coming on leave any day he'll be, and mad to see the baby.'

'Tea, Mrs Furneaux, dear,' said Nurse Howe, slapping the bedtable across Lucy's knees and stopping to look at her. 'Feeling all right?'

'I've got indigestion,' said Lucy quickly. Her mind more than occupied with Thomas, she took four pieces of bread-and-butter and a slice of cake off the tray and ate her way through them while all the awful and embarrassing potentialities of the situation revealed themselves, one after the other, in turn. On and off she giggled. She thought of Thomas's face when he was confronted with both his wives side by side, in adjoining beds. Lucy would have given a lot to see that; but it was finally off the menu; she had gone too far with her maligning of Thomas and now she was committed to a Past with a fair man called Daniel. She began to feel like someone in an early film, tied to the rails before the oncoming express. Whatever happened, whether Thomas could through some agency be warned beforehand, or whether Lucy could contrive to be asleep with the sheet over her face, there she had to stay in bed. Mrs Reed must in any case remain innocent of the fact that she had wedded Lucy's leavings. The awful part was that there was simply no privacy to be had; impossible, with Mrs Reed three yards away, to confide in one of the nurses and get her to snap up Thomas at the entrance doors. Lucy hoped Thomas would have the grace to send his wife a telegram; this she doubted, knowing him; but in any case he could only come within certain hours, and for those periods, Lucy decided, she would have to sleep. Boring it would certainly be, odd it would surely look to everyone else since she had never yet slept during the day, but there it was; it just showed, if any confirmation were needed, that she should never have married Thomas.

The second Mrs Reed must have done some licking into shape when she took over; for Thomas did send a telegram. It came the next morning, and throughout the next day Lucy watched Mrs Reed grow perceptibly younger, less lank and sharp, emerging as an almost pleasing creature. When Lucy had married Thomas, then a clerk in her father's firm, it had taken her no more than three weeks to see through his alluringly dashing manner to their total lack of tastes in common. They had been brought up in different worlds; they had no bonds. Now with the experience of eight years behind her, Lucy began to understand that circumstance and not Thomas had been the trouble; it was in Thomas to be a good husband of a kind, and it seemed he had found the right wife. The second Mrs Reed would like the things he liked, keep his house immaculate, give him all the lace mats and sustaining meals and potted ferns that Lucy had wanted to throw at his head. All Thomas wanted, for his part, was a nice, safe,

affectionate, bourgeois existence; Lucy, with her books, her
Salvador Dali on the bedroom wall, her communist friends
who wore red ties or (even worse) no ties and her desires
for mushrooms cooked in vermouth at two in the morning,
had brought him to the edge of the bohemian abyss. Having
thought this out, Lucy felt a little more amiable towards
Thomas; but not much; she could not forgive the caravan.

The day passed in its pattern. At intervals Lucy said she
felt tired; cursing Thomas, she lay down in the afternoon and
pretended to sleep, so that no one should think it odd if she
slept again from seven till eight. It was not Louis' night for a
visit; there was a late bus only three times a week. Before seven
o'clock and the moment the after-supper routine was over
Lucy dived under the bedclothes, again cursing Thomas, and
composed herself for an hour at least of stale air and ennui.

Few women could have resisted listening, and Lucy was
not one of them; her ears under the sheet were agog for
Thomas's arrival. When his footsteps clipped across the floor
she began to wonder if a discreet look would be possible; but
her decision that it would had no time to be translated into
action before someone landed her an indiscreet, sudden and
hearty slap on the behind.

Lucy was so surprised she sat up. She could not have
glared with more malevolence at Louis if he had been the
as yet absent Thomas himself. 'Chérie,' said Louis mildly,
'I am a surprise. Bernard had to drive in for something official
so I came with him.' Voluble with her fright and thanking
heaven for the French language, Lucy went for him fer-
ociously with one eye on the door; name of a this and that, she

said, everything was now upset; was there then no telephone between the house and the hospital? Let that pass, said Lucy at top speed, in such a crisis there was only one thing to be done; listen, species of turnip, she said, and poured out the crisis in a torrent, with the directions for coping. 'Then you can come back and say Bernard is not yet ready; dis ça en anglais; tu comprends, cochon?'

'Entendu,' said Louis; enjoying himself vastly, saluting her in false farewell, he took himself off to cope.

'There's late Tom is, the devil,' said Mrs Reed quite cheerfully; calm and flowering, she sat up in a pink jacket and looked at the door.

There's lucky for you he's the same unpunctual so-and-so, Lucy said to herself. Having her baby had been nothing to this; she felt even more like someone in a film, untied from the rails almost under the train's wheels; but she trusted Louis.

Thus when Thomas came through the swinging doors into the passage he found himself accosted not by a nurse but by some kind of foreigner in very English tweeds. Thomas gave him a nod and thought to proceed; but no. 'You will come and see your baby, please?' said Louis in as official a voice as his costume allowed. It was not official enough; can't speak English properly, poor cheese, was Thomas's only reaction. 'Well, no, thanks,' he said, 'not yet. I'd rather see my wife first.'

'First one looks at the babies,' said Louis, 'then one sees the wives. In here.'

'No, really, old man, my wife's waiting. Thanks all the same.'

'Please.'

'Oh, *hell*.'

'A quarter past seven, now,' said Mrs Reed to Lucy. 'Give it to him I will when he shows his face. Is it your husband makes you laugh, cariad?'

'Like a drain,' said Lucy. As clearly as if she were there she saw Thomas and Louis in the nursery, surrounded by eight babies in little baskets, having it out. The process was short; in two or three minutes Thomas, rather red, came into the ward and made his way to his wife's bed; his boots slapped self-consciously on the floor. Lucy was now enjoying herself; the situation, she felt, was taking on the qualities of a bedroom farce. Over Mrs Reed's head she caught Thomas's eye. Mrs Reed looked at Thomas, Thomas looked at Lucy, and Lucy made a face. Thomas went redder. Honour thus appeased, Lucy lay back and waited for Louis to return and say his piece.

Thomas's leave was only forty-eight hours, as Lucy had discovered with some relief from his wife; nevertheless it was astonishing how many times he managed to ease himself into the ward during the next day. Authority was blind to husbands on leave. Lucy could see that Mrs Reed was waiting for a chance to introduce her to Thomas, and with matching determination gave her no opening. It seemed to Lucy that she spent most of her time feigning sleep; being conscientious about her acting, she had to go on sleeping for half a day after Thomas's departure. Thomas may have imagined, but it was as well that he did not hear, the things Lucy said about him under the bedclothes; and for all the reading she was getting

through she felt she might with greater profit have filled her suitcase with an oxygen apparatus.

Once Thomas was safely out of the way Lucy's friendship with Mrs Reed increased. Thomas and a feeling for Wales encompassed all they had in common; yet by some trick of temperament they got on together. Lucy had a natural gift of discretion; before long she almost believed in Daniel. With touches of embroidery she built up a creation of his character and appearance which became her private pride. On her eighth day (which everyone thought was her ninth, Lucy by constant repetition having effectively confused them) she got up for a bath; thereafter, at last unconfined, she seemed to merge herself back on the staff. Mrs Reed was out of bed a day later, but somehow remained a patient.

On her twelfth day, since Lucy's mother was there to look after the house, they let her go home. Louis came over with a car to fetch her, waiting in the passage till Lucy's protracted parting with the ward should come to an end. Most of the women by now were new patients; terrified of Sister, who was swabbing, they were shocked at Lucy's facetious air. Lucy, half of the world in her imminent departure, leaned against the end of someone's bed; 'I always thought it was steel wool,' she said, 'but I see it's cotton.' Hitching her still simian baby on one elbow, wearing now though not without constriction her black trousers and a grey jacket, she went out of the ward on the alarmed silence that greeted this reference to Sister's heavy competent hand. Arm-in-arm she and Louis went down the stairs, through the cold hall and out into the sun.

'Cochon,' said Lucy, 'do you know what I've done?'

'What have you done?'

'I've asked Thomas's wife to come and stay.'

'Lucy, sometimes I ask myself, will you ever learn?'

'No,' said Lucy, 'I never will, will I? Quel enfant, hein? C'est ta faute, ça.'

'Ecoute, toi . . .'

Holding the baby and launching into argument again, Lucy got in the car beside Louis and they slid off down the winding drive, out into the country and towards home.

THE MISS

The best kind of experience is the kind that takes on, from the start, the right air of unreality; it is like being in an agreeable dream; anything may happen. Some places, seeming to belong to another world, have this quality, too. But, as a rule, they are not the familiar and ordinary places; not, for instance, a cinema on the outskirts of Bath. It was not until the shadowy female in the next seat shot out of it without the least warning, cried 'Meat! Meat!', fell over Lucy and Louis and disappeared from view, that the evening became anything but orthodox. Lucy and Louis, having seen the main film, were sitting through the supporting piece in a kind of coma, kept in their places partly by lethargy, partly by a disinclination not to get their money's worth since they rarely went to a cinema, and mostly by the fact that each was waiting for the other to say, Let's get out of here. The cry of 'Meat! Meat!' was enough to set them going; they looked at each other, got up in silence, and pushed open the still pulsating doors marked EXIT.

In the pink light of the entrance hall the female was to be seen scuttling out towards the street. She was what Lucy and

Louis called a Miss, which meant not any spinster but a particular kind, and she was dressed genteelly in a grey coat and a mauve hat with a puff of grey feathers, and though her face could not be seen it could easily be imagined. Across the hall she half ran, a little oldish creature, as awkward as a hen.

'Meat,' said Lucy, pulling on her gloves.

'She perhaps leaves it in the oven,' said Louis, 'and forgets it.'

'Some kind of meal seemed to be going on in the film, but I don't remember any meat, do you?'

'I remember not even any meal; but when I am awake and one says to me Food, Lucy, then I think always of meat – une côtelette de veau garnie, ou peut-être des tournedos, ou même un beau morceau de —'

'Ça suffit; not everyone is so carnivorous. For that matter, she might be a vegetarian shooting a protest.'

'Or since in this uncivilised language one can say the same thing with different letters, it may be that she forgets to meet someone, that is to say, rencontrer.'

'Conceivably,' said Lucy, being kind, 'but if you forgot a date, I think you wouldn't, on the whole, be quite so peculiar. You might say "Heavens – Kenneth!" or "My God, the Pump Room nine-fifteen", or probably just "Damnation", but no one but a lunatic would say "Meet! Meet!"'

'Then she is, perhaps, one of those. Or Lucy, when dogs and horses run after the fox that is also a meet, yes?'

'I am always telling you, *hounds*; farmers of all people, even foreign ones, Louis, simply cannot afford to say dogs, not that I care. And after dark in the City of Bath I hardly think a fox-hunt is a very good explanation. Nor was she wearing riding clothes. Forgive me if I am too damping.'

'One must consider everything,' said Louis, undamped. 'But it is clearly the meat in the oven. If you must know, you could ask her because she is there waiting for the bus like a cat on hot feet.'

'Bricks,' said Lucy with automatic persistence, almost without thinking. It was the desert hour of the evening, both too early and too late. The long street, half-empty, bore its narrowing chains of lights away into the distance towards the city. Under the bus-stop sign the Miss fidgeted, irresolute, taking a short run forward, peering back, torn between a certainly fatal period of walking and a probably catastrophic wait. Watching her from the glossy steps littered with bus-tickets, Lucy appeared to come to a decision. 'We could give her a lift,' she said, 'couldn't we? You get the car, Louis, and I can go and pick her up.'

'I think I will like to drop her again soon,' said Louis. 'First one sucks the juice, then one throws away the orange. She is not my type.'

'First meat, and now dessert,' said Lucy. 'Your mind turns in gastronomic cycles. Do try and be a little more English when you drive up; we don't want to put her off.' She crossed the street to the bus stop and offered a lift with the right air of casual philanthropy. The Miss fluttered. Her glasses directed minute beams of the reflected lights on Lucy's bare head, her low-heeled shoes, her black town suit scented only faintly with Vol de Nuit superimposed hopefully on DDT solution. Lucy could see them approving the absence of furs, of heel-spikes, of red nails and diamonds; passed the Lady Test, she thought smugly. 'It would be very kind of you,' said the Miss, 'very kind, indeed. I am really most – the fact is, I forgot that I had – that my maid is out. Everything is bolted, of course, but these days one doesn't like leaving a house empty for long, does one?'

'Most unwise,' said Lucy, who hadn't bolted the front door for years, except when they went on holiday. She added, 'Though it's rather different for us in the country.'

'Oh, you live in the country? Delightful,' said the Miss, seeming surprised.

'My husband is a farmer,' said Lucy, anxious to get this in before Louis appeared and thus give him at least a respectable background. Something solid and bourgeois about farming, she said to herself. With a distant but shattering roar, Louis was to be heard starting the car.

'A beautiful life,' said the Miss. 'I always think the good earth is – and how busy you must be; poultry, I expect, and curing hams and drying herbs, and butter —'

'Well,' said Lucy rather hurriedly, 'I have three small children. My mother is looking after them while we have a few days' holiday here, not holiday exactly because my husband is buying a new tractor, but it's a change.' At this moment, as she was thinking out a remark about the Vicar, Louis, in the ancient Bentley, exploded from the car park and thundered across the road. The hood was down. Louis had wound himself in a vast black woollen scarf and put on his béret; he kept both these articles under the seat, the one in case it was cold and the other for when he greased the car. Lucy gave him a

stony glare. The Miss looked apprehensive. Her eyes turned from Louis (no, it can't be) to the car park (he must be on the way), back to Louis (we are being accosted) and then with increasing doubt to Lucy, who said, 'Do sit in the front, won't you? It's more sheltered and rather cleaner.' The Miss looked more apprehensive than ever, but let herself be coaxed into the front seat; during the coaxing, Lucy managed to give Louis a sharp blow with her elbow, though not as sharp as she could have wished. Louis smiled. Lucy extracted uneasy directions from the Miss, and they roared off down the street.

Lucy knew that Louis was going to do something difficult; she leaned with her elbows on the back of the front seat and began talking about Bath. It was easy to see what the Miss was thinking: Her husband is a farmer; this cannot be a farmer; therefore this cannot be her husband. Driving in silence, Louis waited benignly for a pause in Lucy's conversational flow; when it came, he inclined towards the Miss, turned on her a momentary but intent stare, and said in an unnaturally foreign accent, before Lucy could think up any red herring about the Roman Baths, 'It ees perhaps already now too late – no?'

Appalled, the Miss jerked sideways and looked at him as a rabbit looks at a snake, or as if he had bitten her. She opened her mouth twice and said in a faint voice, 'Too —?'

'For the meat,' said Louis, 'in the oven. It will be burnt, yes?'

The Miss appeared (if that were possible) even more flustered than before. Lucy, running over in her mind the alternatives of a rendezvous and a fox-hunt, suddenly realised

that Louis was suspected of being not only sinister but psychic. 'It isn't second sight,' she said. 'We were sitting next to you in the cinema.'

At this the poor Miss relaxed, though gradually, and still alarmed by Louis. 'How silly of me – I should have known, shouldn't I? So startling – it went right out of my mind and then I remembered in a flash, just like — You see, it's the week's joint, and the weather rather close, isn't it, and my maid being out I put it in the oven to seal it up – I believe that's what one should do – and then I came out and, of course, I quite forgot to . . . How clever of you to have guessed.' Louis, seeming resigned now that he had made his effect, unbent and turned on charm; Lucy watched the Miss disapprove, doubt, hesitate and succumb. As soon as they reached their destination, hindered by little flutters from the front seat ('I could really get down here – well, to the left there is *slightly* quicker, but I'm sorry – oh, you have to go back, oh dear – I *do* hope I'm not taking you out of your . . .'), it became plain that Lucy's irrational impulse had been right; the house was a beauty. It was part of a little crescent half-enclosing a dark garden of trees. War had ripped away the railings of the square but left the houses intact; with the bloom of decay on their smoky-gold stone they were more elegant, more romantic than ever. Now Lucy was filled with a desire to penetrate this dream-like eighteenth-century façade; to drive away would be to wake unnaturally in the middle of the sequence. She unpacked the Miss and fidgeted agonisedly on the kerb. 'How very kind of you,' said the Miss, '– I am so grateful. I do hope – but, of course, you must come in and have some refreshment

– perhaps a glass of wine? No, please – I insist . . .' Wine? said
Louis's eyebrows; he climbed out, with some kind of Contin-
ental murmur. Either home-made elderberry or the best
Tonic, or perhaps Empire Port Type, Lucy said to herself, and
here comes the poor sap expecting Château Lafite; but
she only followed the Miss up the three shallow steps to the
door, without a word to Louis, who in return for his earlier
performance deserved all he got and more.

While the Miss did one of those key-hunting acts without
which Misses never seem able to get into their houses, Lucy
looked down over the railings, which here had been preserved
to stop the inhabitants from breaking their necks, into the
basement area and that of the house next door. Against
the dividing grille of the latter leaned a maid, doing nothing
much, contemplating, perhaps, enjoying the night air or
waiting for the policeman on his beat. All this struck Lucy at
once as rather odd and out-of-date, because those few of her
friends who had domestics at all, instead of girls from the
village or just nothing, seemed to have the current kind who
wear flowered crêpe de Chine and go out dancing five nights
a week with engineers or wireless mechanics. This maid, however, who was not quite middle-aged and had protruding
eyes, wore a uniform and even a cap. The eyes met Lucy's as
she stood above; and the glance, which somehow managed
with no more than a flicker to include the still fumbling Miss,
was accompanied mysteriously by a shake of the head; not
an urgent shake, but one expressing a sort of resigned pity,
entirely incomprehensible to its victim. Lucy did not have
time to think it out, or even to counter with a look of enquiry,

before the front door was opened at last by the Miss and they were all enveloped in a smell of burning so strong that it ought to have been partnered by clouds of black smoke. 'Oh dear,' cried the Miss in anguish, 'oh, I'm afraid – how *could* I have forgotten? Such beautiful meat, too. . . . Perhaps in here it will – no, it isn't very bad if I shut the door quickly. This is my own little sitting-room – I think if I open the window at the top it will – now please sit down and be comfortable and I will just go and turn off the — It won't take a minute. . . .' She shot out, looking crestfallen.

Lucy and Louis lost at once their air of polite concern and began to giggle. 'Oh, I *am* enjoying this,' said Lucy. 'When you came out of the car park I thought we were finished, but now I'll have to forgive you. It's wonderful; it's like a room in a museum.' Round the walls she prowled, inspecting the painted china, the everlasting flowers, the upright piano with pleated silk faded to a mal de mer green behind fretwork panels, the beaded stools and the water-colours, on which pink light spouted from a fringed shade. 'Sacrilege, really,' she said, thinking of the house, 'but how agreeably awful.'

'If it is her house,' said Louis, 'one would think she would not choose so small a room for her own.'

'Some kinds of inferiority complex like to have their elbows confined,' said Lucy.

Louis looked perplexed, took out his pipe, peered into it and guiltily put it back.

'Another thing,' Lucy said, 'did you see that maid in the next-door basement shake her head at me? I can't think what the hell she meant. It might have been Look Out, or just

T-t-t or She Keeps the Safe Locked, or anything. But it doesn't matter,' said Lucy, rushing on to the next idea, 'because I've just remembered what I was trying to think of – she was like the piece in Eliot:

> I am aware of the damp souls of housemaids
> Sprouting despondently at area gates.

Louis thought this over in silence. 'It is poetry, yes?' he said finally.

'Yes.'

'Area,' said Louis after some more thought, 'that is what you call basement, no?'

'Yes,' said Lucy. 'Do take off that scarf.'

'But if it is basement it is that one see their heads and not their feet.'

'No one said anything about feet – you seem to have got it all wrong, with your usual dexterity. Here she is coming back.'

'I am so sorry,' said the Miss, letting herself in along with a strong blast of charred meat, 'so rude to leave you like this. I'm afraid it was burnt right up, but nothing was actually on fire, and I have opened all the — We must hope the smell will blow away. Do please sit down – forgive me for asking,' she said in confidential tones to Lucy, 'but your . . . your husband is not English, is he?'

'He is my husband,' said Lucy, 'but he is French.'

'Indeed! How very – but surely, that is, didn't you say he was a farmer? I thought —'

'One can be a farmer,' said Louis, turning his attention from an anonymous bottle with three glasses on a tray, at

which he had been directing furtive and increasingly appalled glances, 'and be also French. In France I am a farmer. In the war I come here. I am discharged from the air and now I am a farmer in England. One can plough in any language.'

'How unusual and delightful – and do you speak French, too?'

'I have to,' said Lucy, 'or we should never get anywhere.'

'Oh, come, come,' said the Miss, who seemed very much taken with Louis, 'I think your husband's English is really – so attractive, a foreign accent. I know the French like wine, so I have brought up some of my own parsnip – it's three years old and really I am afraid quite potent – now you must both try it. I mustn't be too liberal, must I, because of driving the car. . . .' With a kind of whinny, in which Lucy thought she detected a touch of malice, the Miss bent over inelegantly and filled three glasses with a fluid that reminded Louis at once, though he could not think why and indeed would rather not have dwelt on the idea at all, of the stuff that pickles biological specimens in hospital laboratories. He swallowed and turned his eyes to the pink shade over their heads. 'There now,' said the Miss, and raised her glass reverently. 'La Belle Frongse,' she said.

'Votre santé,' said Lucy, not looking at Louis.

'A bas le War Agricultural Committee,' said Louis, rather late and under his breath, and drained off half his portion.

'I have to keep it locked up,' said the Miss, 'for fear of tempting my maid. It would not be at all good for her – she is a little unbalanced, she has hallucinations. Do you find it very strong?'

'Me, I find it unbelievable,' said Louis politely.

'What sort of hallucinations?' said Lucy, interested.

'It's rather difficult to explain – often she thinks she is someone else, or that I am . . . May I give you some more wine? Do please let me fill up your glass.'

Lucy was about to say how delicious it was but really they ought to be thinking of going, when the front door across the hall was thunderously shut, rattling the Presents from Bournemouth on the mantelpiece, and a tramp like a policeman's began milling around inside. 'Oh *dear*,' said the Miss, 'oh, she has come back early. I thought she would be – no, you mustn't think of going, do have another glass of wine, please let me — This is my private sitting-room, she won't come in here. May I —?'

Lucy was so engrossed in wondering why the maid was unwelcome (most people being only too pleased if their general helps got in unaccompanied and cold sober by the small hours), why it was necessary to insist she wouldn't burst into sitting-rooms, and why she wore Army boots, that she found her glass filled up before she could muster any excuse. Louis, more concerned with his stomach than with mad domestics, got off by saying, 'Thank you, but no, I am not to be tempted, it is that when I drink I drive not so good.' On Lucy he turned a private and anguished glance, but Lucy took no notice. 'Good *Lord*!' said Army Boots from the hall. The Miss looked anxiously at the door, clasping the parsnip bottle round its neck, making a kind of weak rescue bid, 'I think perhaps —' but Lucy never knew what thoughts of flight through the window or crawlings under the table were in her mind, for into the middle of the sentence burst another Miss, an enormous one, dressed in felt, tweeds and ankle-boots, and in a state of belligerent alarm, crying, 'Good Lord, Marian, *not* the joint? Is the house on fire again? *Really*, it's too sickenin' —'

'Everything's all right, do please be calm, Amelia,' said the Miss, far from calm herself but fired, perhaps, by two glasses of parsnip wine. 'It did get a little burnt, but I remembered – I was in the cinema and monsieur very kindly drove me home. . . .'

'Monsieur?'

'Madame,' said Louis, misunderstanding and politely bowing.

'Monsieur is French,' said the Miss unnecessarily. Seeing endless complications ahead, and told by her sense of timing that the right moment had come, Lucy got up firmly and said, 'Thank you so much for the drink, it was delightful; but I'm afraid we shall really have to go now.'

'Oh, please don't, must you really? It's only about half past – you mustn't let Amelia drive you away; she has the privileges of an old retainer, you know,' said the Miss, dropping her voice, but not far enough.

'Marian,' roared Army Boots, 'kindly remember your place. There's such a thing as goin' too far. You'd better start clearin' up; *I* will show your friends out.'

'Well, goodbye, and thank you,' said Lucy, asking herself whether this was a private house or a lunatic asylum; from the calmness with which Louis conducted his rather baroque leave-taking, she gathered that he was merely accepting

the home ground eccentricities of the sort of English Type familiar throughout France before the war, the finer points of lunacy being lost on him. He took in the broad outline; details were not to be bothered with. The English Misses are mad; ça suffit. One remains polite.

Army Boots tramped through the hall and reminded Lucy of Kipling. 'Very kind of you to bring my maid back,' she said. Lucy saw Louis open his mouth; she kicked him. 'Glad she asked you in. She's a trifle unbalanced, as you can see; embarrassin', but no harm in it; anyway, you can't pick and choose these days. There it is; I'm grateful. Mind the steps. Good night to you both.'

Lucy was somehow faintly surprised to see the car still there; a street-lamp threw a circle of light round it, across the pavement, and up the lovely front of the house. It shone, too, on the next-door maid, who now stood leaning against the railings at the top of the area steps.

'Lucy,' said Louis, 'I think I have not understood who is what.'

'I'll be frank with you,' said Lucy. 'I think I haven't, either.'

'Quite easy,' said the next-door maid. 'They're both dotty, see?'

Irresistibly drawn, Lucy found herself beside the steps instead of in the car. 'Well, whose house is it?' she said. She would by now not have been surprised to be answered, Mine: I'm the Duchess of Bath.

The maid cast a resigned eye upwards; the other, being, Lucy decided, of glass, stayed disconcertingly fixed on her. 'They shares it,' she said, 'but they each pretends it's theirs.'

Her gaze reunited. 'Had to get the firemen in twice. She leaves something in the oven nearly every week, Miss Marian does. They thinks it's nice, see, pretending they each got a maid; gives them something to think about, like. Cor, look out,' she said, and melted away competently. Out of the front door, down the three steps, pattered the Miss, guilty and short of breath.

'Do forgive me,' she said, 'I just wanted to thank you again and apologise for Amelia – I told you, you know – when she has one of her spells she's liable to burst in like that. I do hope you didn't mind. Perhaps if you are still in Bath you could come and see me Thursday afternoon – she goes out on Thursdays to — I should so enjoy it. . . . Well, bonswar – or shall I say au revwar? I'm so grateful. . . .'

'We'd love to, if we're still here,' said Lucy. She could not help a sideways glance at the area steps. They were empty.

'Were you talking to that maid next door?' said the Miss. 'She always tries to get into conversation. She's not quite . . . you know. . . .' Impaled on Lucy's and Louis's fascinated gaze, she tapped her forehead with one finger. 'Oh yes,' said Lucy.

'MARIAN!' bellowed Army Boots from within.

'*Good*bye,' cried the Miss. She tossed her head defiantly and watched them drive away.

At the corner of the crescent Louis braked. 'My béret; I leave it there.'

'Do you want to go back?' said Lucy. Louis meditated, sighed, and drove on.

'What a lovely evening,' said Lucy. 'Wasn't it heaven?'

'The domestic,' Louis said, 'in the basement; I look at her feet. They are quite dry. They do not sprout.'

'Sprout? Why should they?' said Lucy, thinking of something else. 'You sound as dotty as the Misses. I expect by now they're boiling your béret in a cauldron with a snail's liver and someone's thumb.'

'Comment?' said Louis, disbelievingly.

Lucy said it again. Louis slowed the car and peered at her. 'It is confectious,' he said. 'My God, but yes. We get away from here quickly.' He put his foot down on the accelerator.

ANNABEL'S MOTHER

Every year, as soon as they arrived, they wondered why they had come to the same place again. Sitting on the edge of the same bed, in the room the hotel always gave them, Mrs Keven had to remind herself what holidays would be like alone in the flat with Annabel. She told herself how nice it was to be able to get away and meet new people; how pleasant not to be tied down to a family party at Christmas, an aunt to stay at Easter; how good for Annabel, a change and sea air to set her up for the hot weather she disliked.

Since Mr Keven had died, five years ago when Annabel was seven, Mrs Keven had never spent a school holiday in solitary confinement with her daughter. She tried to imagine herself decorating a tree in the flat at Christmas, playing games with Annabel; at Easter dyeing the egg ration pink, in the summer taking spam sandwiches on the Common to sit by the lake. But it was no good; she couldn't. Those diversions were for people whose children were companions, dependants. Annabel was a governess.

Annabel stood looking out of the window with her nose on the glass, at the thin spring sun on the sea, the sea curling in the high, cold spring wind. 'Mummy,' she said, 'do you know why there's an extra high tide today?'

'No, dear.'

'Mummy, you *are* dull; don't you really know?'

'No, dear; why?'

'It's because of the moon.'

'I think we'd better start unpacking.'

'Mummy, don't you *want* to learn?'

'Yes, darling, of course; it's very interesting. There's such a draught here. Let's get unpacked and go downstairs.'

'I'd like to go out to Boots and change my book,' said Annabel. 'I've finished it. They won't have shut yet, will they? Unless you'd like to read it first. It's about a man who went from Dakar to Nairobi in an Austin Seven.'

'No, thank you, dear, I don't think so; you change it.'

'Well, it *is* rather difficult.'

Mrs Keven sat in the lounge, knitting a blue cardigan in cable stitch for Annabel. Two oldish spinsters, who had been there last Easter and the one before, nodded at her from across the hearth, entrenched in their conversation about the reconstruction of Germany. Two married couples played contract in silent fury, and in the corner by the window a man sat reading. Mrs Keven, inexpert at bridge and reconstruction, looked at him over her knitting. He was a few years older than she, thirty-eight, perhaps, or forty; his clothes were untidy, his face bony and aquiline with receding hair, his mouth large and appealing, his eyes dark. She twisted her head on one side and narrowed her eyes to read the title of his book: Shaw's *The Quintessence of Ibsenism*. Oh dear, thought Mrs Keven; oh well.

Probably waiting for his wife, she said to herself.

'Why you should have thought I had the ace of hearts —' said one half of one of the married couples.

'But the real point is,' said the younger spinster, 'are the Germans *capable* of democracy?'

Annabel came through the glass doors from the sea front, her hair blown about, her face pink with the wind, carrying a large book. She sat on the arm of Mrs Keven's chair. 'Mummy, look, don't you think this ought to be nice? It's about Van Gogh.'

'Yes, dear, very nice; and with pictures too.'

'Mummy, don't you know who Van Gogh *was*?'

'Darling, I forget; who was he?'

'But Mummy, you must have heard of him. Didn't you ever do art at school?'

'It's nearly twenty years since I went to school. I'm going to have a bath now.'

'Oh, *Mummy*! He was a Dutch painter. He went and worked with the miners in Belgium, and then he went to Paris and painted, and then he went to the South of France, and once he cut off his ear and sent it to a girl. Mummy, are you listening?' Annabel followed her mother out of the lounge, discoursing on Van Gogh in her clear and penetrating young voice. As they passed the window the man in the armchair looked up and met Mrs Keven's eyes; he gave her a faint ironic smile; Mrs Keven blushed. On her way through the hall she stopped and opened the visitors' book. Mr and Mrs Leach, Captain and Mrs Holbrook, Miss Scott-Preame, Miss ffoulkes, Dr E Ferris. Of London. There were no other Ferrises. Mrs

Keven went on up the staircase, followed by Annabel saying something about Gauguin and yellow chairs; she wasn't listening.

Since last Easter the dining-room had been painted; someone had worked round to the notion that light green was more cheerful than dark brown. Mrs Keven wore her black frock with a small white pointed collar, which she had some-how meant to keep for Easter Sunday, and had pinned at the neck the diamond clip Julian had given her for a wedding present. She looked critically across the table at her child, wishing Annabel's mouth were bigger, her hair less straight, granting her the beauty of Julian's large grey eyes and dark lashes. Mrs Keven's own eyes were long and narrow, and the colour, Julian had always said laughing, of beer. 'Annabel,' she said in sudden half-absent irritation, 'don't push your hair behind your ears like that. It makes me think of rabbits.'

'Oh, Mummy, how can I tell you about Doctor Banting if you keep on talking about my hair? Don't you want to know how he found insulin?'

'Yes, of course, dear; how?'

Annabel launched off. Over the vase of daffodils Mrs Keven felt Ferris's eyes on them; she looked at her plate.

In the lounge after dinner Annabel sat on a stool beside her mother's chair, reading the life of Van Gogh in temporary silence. Mrs Keven knitted and drank her coffee; the married couples, on bidding but hardly speaking terms, began another rubber; by the fire Miss ffoulkes and Miss Scott-Preame discussed National Insurance; Ferris, his long legs crossed, read Shaw on Ibsen.

'Mummy,' said Annabel, 'it's awfully interesting about the Borinage. Shall I tell you?'

'Yes, darling, but don't make a noise. You'll disturb people.'

Annabel began. Mrs Keven, for the hundredth time, wished children's voices were less emphatic. There was apparently a great deal to be said about the Borinage, whatever the Borinage was, a vital fact she seemed to have missed. She put down her knitting, wondering how soon she could send Annabel to bed, and looked in her bag for a cigarette.

'Don't waste matches,' said Ferris; stretching a long arm from his chair, he clicked an enormous utilitarian steel lighter. Mrs Keven, blushing, said 'Thank you so much.' Annabel broke off and looked at him coldly. 'Do go on,' said Ferris. 'Is that your school homework for holidays?'

'No,' said Annabel. 'I like books. What are you reading?'

'One about Ibsen. Do you know who Ibsen was?'

'Oh yes. He wrote plays; he was Swedish.'

'Norwegian,' said Ferris.

Annabel went red; Mrs Keven gave him a look half-admiring, half-pleading. 'I meant Norwegian,' said Annabel. She added defiantly, 'He wrote a play called *The Wild Goose*.'

'Duck,' said Ferris. '*The Wild Duck*.'

Crimson, Annabel got up and said to her mother, 'I think I'll go and read in bed.'

'Do, dear,' said Mrs Keven with faint apprehension, 'you've had a tiring day. Wash properly and don't forget your teeth. I shan't be very long.'

'No, don't be,' said Annabel. 'I'll tell you the rest in bed.'

She kissed her mother, looked at and through Ferris, and walked with a touch of unwonted self-consciousness out of the lounge.

Ferris took a cigarette from a disintegrating leather case, saying thoughtfully, 'She seems to have a vast store of general knowledge.'

'The thing is,' said Mrs Keven, 'I can't trip her up; I'm so glad you managed to. You've sown the seed of doubt in my mind about whether she *is* always as right as she seems to be, which does give me a sort of confidence. Not, of course, that I shall ever know; but it's nice to see her shaken.'

'But it's a good thing, objectively, this desire for knowledge; not enough people have it. It's the method that gets you down, isn't it?'

'It seems to me it's not so much wanting to know for the sake of knowing as wanting to know so she can tell people who don't,' said Mrs Keven incoherently.

'But she's very young.'

'Well, I'm sorry she was rude; that's because she just isn't used to being corrected. I'm afraid they don't even correct her at school, as far as I can make out. It's a sort of progressive school,' said Mrs Keven dismally; 'her father was very keen on progressive education. I often feel it's not the right sort of place for Annabel, but I don't know enough about other kinds to take her away, and I've no doubt he knew best, really.' Finding herself talking thus freely to a stranger, she stopped and blushed.

But Ferris was serious over the problem of Annabel; he sat frowning gently in his chair. 'It's important you shouldn't have a feeling of inferiority; that's very bad for her, I think. You must try to correct her sometimes.'

'I can't,' said Mrs Keven. 'Truly I can't. I don't know anything.'

'Nothing at all?' said Ferris, his long mouth smiling. 'Get an encyclopaedia and look up things she doesn't know, ask her them and tell her the answers. But don't let it worry you. Somehow I can't quite believe in your ignorance, anyway.'

'Oh, it's true,' said Mrs Keven. 'My husband married me because I knew nothing; he liked to impart knowledge.' She broke off and blushed again. But once started she could not stop talking to Ferris; his manner of listening invited confidence. Miss ffoulkes and Miss Scott-Preame faded away upstairs, the bridge four parted at last, and still Ferris and Mrs Keven went on about Annabel.

Only when Mrs Keven went to bed, feeling for things in the dark for fear of waking her child who would begin to talk, did she realise that all she knew of Ferris was that his wife was dead.

Annabel's policy in the morning seemed to be to ignore Ferris and the Ibsen incident. The latter was not difficult; but it was less easy to pretend Ferris was not there. Annabel was occupied with the beach and spent much time in the bookshop; when as arranged she went to meet her mother for coffee in the small cakeshop facing the sea she found Ferris there too; across a table in the very olde-worlde bow window they were deep in a conversation that broke off when she came in, and had been, Annabel at once suspected, about her. Sitting between them gloomily eating cakes, watching spray dashed by the wild spring wind against the olde-worlde glass, she said as little as she could to Ferris, and sulked that he would not try to make her talk. A gradual and annoyed surprise took hold of her, hearing Ferris with every appearance of interest asking her mother questions, hearing her mother answer with every appearance of competence and sureness. Annabel could see no reason why Ferris should want to know about the merits of gas and electric cookers, the Government's provisions for children, how welfare clinics worked and what shopping conditions had been like during the war; but it was odd to hear her mother, instead of saying 'I don't know, dear; how?' launch into a reasoned account of each subject. Still, it's her job, thought Annabel; peevishly she stretched a hand for her fourth cake. On the way home she turned into a shop; Ferris and Mrs Keven went ahead back to the hotel.

'Mummy,' said Annabel in their room before lunch, 'is that man going to be here all the time?' She looked accusingly in the mirror at Mrs Keven, who was sitting in front of it pinning up her curly dark-brown hair over her ears in a new way.

'Till we go tomorrow week,' said Mrs Keven. 'He has to leave the same day.' She was not apologetic; indeed her manner was almost pert.

'I don't like him,' said Annabel, after waiting vainly to be asked.

'Don't you, dear?'

Annabel said unwillingly, 'What does he do?'

'He's in medical research.'

Appearing to take no notice, Annabel loafed around the room, tapping the drops of rain on the window, unscrewing the lid of her mother's cold-cream jar and screwing it down again. At last she said, 'Mummy, there's a little book in Davis's I thought I might get. It's about hydroponics.'

'I should, dear,' said Mrs Keven. She wondered vaguely whether she ought to have said, 'You're too young to read about that sort of thing.'

'Do you know what hydroponics are, Mummy?'

'Dearest, I've no idea.'

'Well, don't you *want* to know anything? Mummy, you really ought to make efforts.'

'Well, what are they?'

'Mummy, haven't you honestly ever *heard* of hydroponics?'

'Never,' said Mrs Keven, contentedly fiddling with her curls.

'It's a new science,' said Annabel, 'growing things in tanks without any earth. You grow them in water with chemicals in it, and you don't need nearly so much room because you can do it in layers, and they grow more quickly. It's going to cause an agricultural revolution.'

'Darling, it's fascinating,' said Mrs Keven.

Mollified, Annabel brushed her hair once on each side, wiped her hands with her mother's face flannel and the clean towel, and went down to lunch.

The next day another guest arrived: she was a small dark girl in the uniform of a WAAF officer, with blue eyes, black smooth hair brushed up on her head, and a skin like Chinese porcelain. Annabel hung around anxiously, waiting to see if

Ferris would speak to her. After dinner she went into the lounge with the book on hydroponics (which had proved both technical and boring but remained impressive in appearance) and found Ferris and the little WAAF in armchairs three yards apart, engaged in desultory talk about local scenery. Annabel ran up to the bedroom, where Mrs Keven was catching up a hole in her best silk stockings. She began to loaf and fiddle. In due course she said, 'Mummy, don't you think that Air Force girl is awfully pretty?'

'Air Force what?' said Mrs Keven, not attending.

'Mummy, don't you even *notice* anything? The one who came this afternoon.'

'Oh, that one; yes, dear, very.'

'She's sitting next to Doctor Ferris in the lounge,' said Annabel casually, 'talking.'

'Is she? Annabel, do leave my cream alone. It's so scarce.'

'They're sitting quite close together, too.'

'Sometimes I wonder if you're twelve or six,' said Mrs Keven with amiable disinterest. Annabel reddened and slammed down the jar of cream. She went out of the room.

On Easter Sunday the weather became calm, the heavenly thin bright sun of spring threw flashes of light on the sea. Mrs Keven wore her black frock and an absurd and fetching bracelet of copper plaques and green glass beads that Annabel had given her for Christmas, and walked in the salt sunlight along the promenade with her child, thinking how dreary the last holidays had been and asking herself whether uncongenial company had made them dismal or whether the hotel had improved out of all recognition. Annabel was going on about poetry. From long experience Mrs Keven made the right remarks; but she walked in a trance, unhearing.

Long after dinner, when Annabel had gone to bed, Ferris said to her, 'I had an almost normal talk with the problem child while you were upstairs. Doesn't that surprise you?'

'No talk with Annabel could be quite normal,' said Mrs Keven; 'what about?'

'Medical science, by way of hydroponics. She told me a lot, but she did ask me a question.'

'What – "Doctor Ferris, don't you *want* to learn?"'

'I seemed to avoid that one. It was about dissecting cats.'

'By the time we leave, if you go on at this rate, she'll be almost a normal child.'

Ferris said, 'Do you think we could meet sometimes in London? I'd like to know how she gets on.'

'That would be very nice,' said Mrs Keven, for once without blushing.

Annabel, lying awake in bed while her mother undressed, said, 'Mummy, do you know how they find out whether cats have got TB?'

'No, dear,' said Mrs Keven. 'And I don't want to,' she added firmly. 'Do you like Doctor Ferris any better?'

'No. At least, not much. But he knows a lot.'

'We're going to meet him in London sometimes.'

'Well, you can; I don't want to. He thinks Miss Jordan in the Air Force is very pretty,' said Annabel maliciously.

'So would anyone,' said Mrs Keven, getting into bed.

In the week after Easter and before their departure Annabel managed a gloomy politeness towards Ferris. Once or twice they had coldly technical discussions about science, in which Ferris did most of the talking and Annabel absorbed information looking as though she already knew it. Whether Ferris ever said anything to Annabel about her relationship with her mother Mrs Keven could not decide; but it seemed to her that in the last few days Annabel's lectures were not quite so frequent, perhaps a shade less intellectual and contemptuous. In Ferris's company Mrs Keven was entirely happy; his impersonal interest, his objective judgements, pleased her in spite of a touch of practical frustration. For by then Mrs Keven was asking herself whether one day she might not marry Ferris; and in his presence she saw no foundation of reason for expecting it.

In a state of vague depression she did the packing on the morning they were to leave. Annabel hindered her by fiddling with things and talking about Mendel and white rats; every so often she said 'Mummy, are you listening?'

'Yes, dear,' said Mrs Keven.

'Well, what did I say?'

'Darling, do be quiet; I'm trying to concentrate. Where are your pyjamas?'

When the suitcases were shut and strapped Annabel said, 'Mummy, is he coming in the train with us?'

'I expect so,' said Mrs Keven distractedly. 'He said he'd meet us at the station.'

'Why at the station?'

'Oh heavens, I forget; something about a book.'

'Mummy, you really ought to try and think clearly.'

A cold April wind blew relentlessly on the platform. Mrs

Keven, holding fiercely on to the black felt saucer which Annabel said made her look fast, screwed up her eyes to catch sight of Ferris's gaunt shape among the departing guests; but he was not to be seen. On this branch line the train, till it reached the junction, was comparatively empty; by going diligently right up to the front they found a carriage to themselves. Mrs Keven would not look out of the window, but sat sternly in a corner, taking off her hat with an air of desolate indifference, tidying her hair. Annabel lounged opposite with one foot on the seat. She said nothing, but looked with increasing hope towards the door of the compartment. No one came in; and in due course the train started.

Annabel put up both her feet and leaned back. 'Mummy,' she said, 'I expect he decided to come on a later one.'

'Probably,' said Mrs Keven.

'Or he might have missed it.'

Mrs Keven made no reply.

'Anyway,' said Annabel, becoming annoyed at not being noticed, 'he was talking to the WAAF when we left. I expect he's going to travel with her.'

'Take your feet off the seat and sit up,' said Mrs Keven. Her eyelids began to smart and sting with what could not now be passed off as the cold wind on the platform; the conviction grew on her that her feelings were getting out of control. She sat looking out of the window and waiting for the smart to subside; it didn't. She had to get up and say to Annabel, in a voice that thank heaven seemed to sound all right, 'I'm going along to do my hair properly; I can't see in my compact mirror.'

When she had gone Annabel put her feet back on the seat and felt in the pocket of her reefer coat for the toffee she had bought on the way to the station, the last of her ration guarded for the journey; chewing, she stared out at the flat dispiriting countryside with defiant satisfaction. Without turning her head she began to scowl. The door from the corridor slid back.

'Almost missed it,' said Ferris, heaving his suitcase on to the rack. 'I got on at the back, and of course you would be at the front. Where's your mother?'

'In the lavatory,' said Annabel ungraciously, 'doing her hair. She's in a state because she thought you weren't coming.'

'Is she, now,' said Ferris, pleased. He took out a cigarette and eyed Annabel reflectively. Annabel stared back, pushing out her lip. After a pause she said: 'Are you going to be my stepfather?'

'I shouldn't be at all surprised.'

'That's what I thought,' said Annabel. 'I thought you didn't really like Miss Jordan enough.'

'Who would Miss Jordan be when she's at home?'

'That WAAF you talked to.'

'WAAF? Oh yes; that one. No, I didn't like her nearly enough; not nearly. Listen, Annabel; when your mother comes back I think it would be a good idea if you went and aired yourself off in the corridor.'

'Do you?' said Annabel. 'Why?'

'Because I say so; or if you prefer it you can stay here and we shall go in the corridor. It makes no difference, frankly, as long as you're somewhere else.'

'When you're my stepfather,' said Annabel, 'are you going to boss me around worse than this?'

'Much worse,' said Ferris happily.

Annabel went red. Sitting facing each other across the carriage, Annabel glaring at Ferris with the forgotten toffee bulging her cheek, Ferris half-smiling at Annabel with resolute good temper, they waited for Mrs Keven to come back.

THE BLUE VASE

On Thursdays, Miss Ledwitch went to Willowplace to play bridge with Miss Pennyfield, Miss Howell and poor Mrs Greene. As Miss Pennyfield hardly ever went out, the parties were always at her house. They provided a weekly afternoon of somewhat masochistic pleasure; what with post-mortems, differences of opinion, and remarks with stings in their tails, it could hardly be called enjoyment at all, except in the case of Mrs Greene, whose standards were lower. At the age of forty-one, Mrs Greene had married a schoolmaster aged fifty-four, seizing the last hope of male protection and company that seemed to be going – how rash and indiscreet a hope had been proved when he had first begotten a child and then collided with a lorry. Left with her own income of two hundred pounds a year and an infant of seven months, Mrs Greene was now worse off than before. She liked going to Miss Pennyfield's once a week because it was an outing. She did her best with the importance of marriage and childbirth, but it was no use, as the others made it plain she was to be pitied rather than looked up to for such experiences.

As for Miss Ledwitch and Miss Howell, they went because they imagined they liked bridge and because they got a kick out of making digs at each other and at Miss Pennyfield. Miss Ledwitch thought Miss Howell was rough and unfeminine and over-sure of herself, and Miss Howell thought Miss Ledwitch was a pussy. No one else in the village played contract so they were forced on one another's company. Miss Ledwitch and Miss Howell went once a month to the village drives, but there the game was auction, which they felt was beneath them, and as they were liable to rush in at the one level with pre-emptive bids of Four Hearts or Five Diamonds, they were understandably not very popular.

Miss Pennyfield was an odd old woman. She lived in a long and low dark-red house built in the marshes outside the village, and the little river ran through her property, which was extensive and quite uncultivated. The rich turf grown with kingcups and willows lapped against her walls. Often on winter evenings when the bridge party broke up, there would be layers of white mist outside, curling around the door, across the meadows. Yet the house, surprisingly, was not damp. It was over-full of old and lovely furniture without even the ghost of bloom or mould on the chestnut polish of the wood. The rooms were dark and peculiarly oblong; in the morning-room where they played bridge, it was almost like sitting in a corridor. Miss Pennyfield had several eccentricities, of which the most marked was a passion for wild animals. Some of her protégés came indoors. Once a hedgehog had brushed Miss Ledwitch's ankle under the bridge table. Miss Ledwitch had screamed, infuriating Miss Howell, who was trying to make a

small slam in hearts. In spite of the wildlife and the dotty way Miss Pennyfield talked to and about it, Miss Ledwitch continued to visit her on Thursdays. She took a perverted pleasure in the torments of bridge; she liked a good tea; and most of all she enjoyed the anguish of sitting there and coveting Miss Pennyfield's blue vase.

Miss Ledwitch had a highly developed property instinct. She could not look on anything that pleased her, from the Mona Lisa to a box with shells on the lid, without a savage desire to possess it. Fortunately, not many things did appeal to her, so there was more room to move in her cottage than one might have expected. Miss Pennyfield's vase was one of the things. Every Thursday, Miss Ledwitch sat through a little private hell of her own, on top of the knocks she got from Miss Howell for not doubling or not unblocking or not taking her out of a psychic, on top of Miss Pennyfield's gibberings about her friends the water-rats, on top of Mrs Greene's dispirited digs about the privileges of motherhood. Instead of seizing the chance to stare placidly at the vase, she simply sat on the mahogany chair seething with frustration because it was not (and nor did it appear likely that it ever would be) hers.

It stood in the middle of the mantelpiece, flanked by a rabble of more or less valuable objects for which Miss Ledwitch did not care a straw. Strictly speaking, it was not a vase but an urn, with two handles and a lid, and a thick and lustrous but dull glaze, in colour a delectable powder-blue patterned with little engraved gilt stars. Each handle was a lusciously baroque cherub clinging with one hand and one foot, all ivory and coral curves and gilt wings, and dressed (but with perfect discretion) in nothing but a scrap of blue porcelain ribbon. The lid was a third cherub, kneeling obligingly with bent head so that he could be lifted off by the wings. Miss Ledwitch could not take her eyes away from it. They swivelled agonisedly towards the mantelpiece every time she came into the room.

One day in late autumn, when the light was already fading and they were playing the last hand before tea, Miss Ledwitch found herself sitting facing the fireplace with nothing to do. She was dummy; Miss Pennyfield was dealing with a contract of Six Spades, which she would make. One of Miss Pennyfield's peculiarities, in view of her wild animals, her eccentric conversation and her refusal to go outside the grounds, was an astonishing competence at bridge. Miss Ledwitch was looking past Miss Pennyfield's intent, rubbery-shapeless face under its meringue of grey hair, down the narrow room to where the vase, catching glints of firelight, seemed to float on the darkening air. She was resolving to ask Miss Pennyfield about it, when the Six Spades were in the bag. She had never mentioned it before. Her eyes were jellied with preoccupation; her mouth was open and her false teeth gleamed.

'– Don't you agree, partner?' said Miss Pennyfield loudly and irritably.

Miss Ledwitch jumped. She blinked to bring the table into focus and saw thirteen tricks mathematically laid along its edge. 'I'm so sorry,' she said. 'Oh yes, indeed. A grand slam, too. What a pity. I was —'

'Only six were there. Miss Howell kindly threw away a diamond instead of a club.'

'So nice to make them all,' said Miss Ledwitch. The moment was almost gone. 'I was admiring your beautiful vase,' she said quickly.

'The blue one with the cherubs? My dear mother —' But Miss Pennyfield's attention was distracted. 'Oh, look,' she cried, 'there is my darling, darling Ricci! Isn't he an angel?' The others turned their heads to the French windows and saw a colossal hare sitting erect in the grass a yard or two outside, in an alert but complacent manner. Miss Howell drew a breath and narrowed her eyes along an imaginary gun. Her finger contracted on an unseen trigger. 'Blessum,' murmured Mrs Greene dutifully. 'The lovely thing!' said Miss Pennyfield, leaning forward. 'No one but a lout, a *vandal*, could destroy a creature like that!' This was another slap at Miss Howell, who was often to be seen striding around in her tweeds with a sporting rifle, dangling limp rabbits by their hind legs. Everyone but Miss Ledwitch had forgotten the blue vase.

Next week I'll ask her again, she thought, when they left at six o'clock. It was dark; in the ray of Miss Howell's torch they waded knee-deep in mist down the path. Mrs Greene hurried on, bound to a timetable by the demands of her infant, who was looked after by a neighbour on Thursdays. Miss Ledwitch and Miss Howell were bound by nothing but their inclinations; these, however, did not prompt them to linger. 'That blasted hare,' said Miss Howell. Next week, thought Miss Ledwitch. They parted briskly, without regret.

But by next week Miss Pennyfield was past telling Miss Ledwitch anything about the blue vase. She had a stroke after lunch on Sunday, and died on Monday morning at twenty minutes to six.

Miss Ledwitch was shocked and astounded. She was careful to point out to herself that shock and surprise had been her first emotions, and that the fate of the blue vase came later, and that much later still came the realisation that they would now have to choose between the evils of three-handed contract and auction. She found, indeed, that she had been rather fond of Miss Pennyfield. She sent her a wreath of white chrysanthemums, and blew her nose hard and often; but she could not go to the funeral, because Miss Pennyfield was rather mysteriously taken off to London for the final ceremony.

When the shock had worn off, Miss Ledwitch went back to the problem of the blue vase. By discreet questioning she at last discovered there was to be an auction sale. All she had to do was to wait with as much patience as she could manage. Every few days she moved the brass clock from the middle of the mantelpiece (which, like most of the immovable parts of her sixteenth-century cottage, consisted of an enormous beam; her infrequent visitors were always being half-stunned) and sat back in one of her heavily-timbered chairs, stifling her conscience and imagining the vase in what she told herself had always been its rightful place. Time passed slowly, in spite of these activities on the part of the clock. Over a month went by before the day arrived. It was wet; but all the same, Miss Ledwitch put on her best black coat, impelled perhaps by another pang of conscience. For the first time in her life she went to Willowplace for a purpose other than contract bridge.

The house looked gloomy and devastated, and gave her a feeling of guilt. The furniture was piled in unfamiliar places and strange, hulking men in damp overcoats tramped mud into the naked floors. The fireplaces were empty. Oh, goodness, oh, dear, thought Miss Ledwitch; oh, poor Miss Pennyfield, what *would* she have said? She pressed her handbag against her stomach, and the pound notes, the subscription to Miss Pennyfield's betrayal, crackled like thorns. Nevertheless, she edged into the morning-room. The vase was in its usual place; a square of white paper, bearing a number, was stuck blasphemously on its front. Miss Ledwitch reached it, and there she stood for an hour and a half, till the tide swept down from the bedrooms, out of the dining-room, and engulfed her in its flow. She bought the vase for two pounds five. Someone at the back was bidding against her; she could not see who it was. Miss Ledwitch, however, had brought ten pound notes in her bag. The opponent dropped out.

She carried it home in her arms and set it in the waiting space on the mantelpiece. There, even more than in Miss Pennyfield's morning-room, it seemed to float on the dark, like a bright and ravishing funeral urn in a vision. The disintegration of Willowplace had made Miss Ledwitch uneasy; she supposed that was why her mind kept running on funeral urns. Also she found it difficult to believe the vase was now really hers. She said to herself, I expect I need a cup of tea. Before she went to put the kettle on, she lifted it down again, to look at it closely and handle it and convince herself it was there. She took the kneeling cherub by his gilt wings and laid

him on the table, and peered through the dark hole at a soft, flaking, chalky bed of ashes.

Miss Ledwitch gave a short scream and leaped backwards. Her teeth clicked, she stared at the vase like a rabbit confronted with a snake, and finally she sank into one of her chairs. After the first moment of blankness her mind, like the vacuum abhorred by nature, sucked in a confusion of ideas that sorted out gradually into the question WHOSE? Miss Ledwitch did not for a moment doubt that the vase contained a Who and not a What; it was, now she came to think of it, just the sort of thing Miss Pennyfield would do. She then remembered how, when she had asked about the vase, Miss Pennyfield had started to say 'My dear mother . . .' Miss Ledwitch cursed the interrupting hare; she would have given much to know what was to have followed. 'My dear mother gave it to me'? or 'My dear mother bought it in Italy'? or – Miss Ledwitch shuddered slightly – 'My dear mother is inside'? The obvious reaction of anyone more gross and material in nature would, of course, be to tip the contents out and forget about them; but Miss Ledwitch, as she was fond of telling anyone who failed to make an escape in time, suffered from over-sensitivity. The very thought of tossing Miss Pennyfield's mother into a corner of the garden made her turn pale and lean her head on one hand. Or even, for that matter, a grandfather; Miss Ledwitch could just as easily imagine Miss Pennyfield saying, 'My dear mother kept her father in it.' And then, worst of all, she remembered Miss Pennyfield's mysterious funeral in London instead of at the village church. Though it seemed on the face of it unlikely and

even eccentric to be expensively cremated in London and then be simply thrown in, as a kind of bonus, with a two-pounds-five vase at a village auction sale, Miss Ledwitch could not put any such behaviour past Miss Pennyfield; she was quite capable of leaving directions in a secret drawer for her ashes to be scattered among the wildlife on the estate. What with all these horrid surmises, Miss Ledwitch was beginning to feel quite ill. In one respect, anyway, she was adamant; living in her cottage with Miss Pennyfield or her mother or grandfather interred on the mantelpiece was something she could not and would not do. With an effort, wearing a horrified, reverent and distasteful air, she picked up the kneeling cherub and put him back in his place. She opened an oak cupboard and shut the vase inside and locked the door, and went, with trembling knees, into the kitchen to make some tea.

Though imaginary vases floated in dark corners for some days, the real one stayed shut up in the cupboard. Miss Ledwitch's disappointment was great; but even after the first shock had passed she could not (being so sensitive) dissociate the container from the contained. She pottered abstractedly, shaking her head often. At the end of the week she answered the rattle of her brass fox's-head knocker on the oak door, and there was Mrs Mead who did such good work for the church. 'Oh, you haven't forgotten, have you, dear?' cried Mrs Mead, '– the things for the jumble sale. Tomorrow, you know; I thought as I was passing —'

Miss Ledwitch started to say 'Indeed, yes, of course . . .' but stopped, and gave Mrs Mead a long, intent and somehow disconcerting look. '*Anything* will do,' said Mrs Mead uneasily.

'Books, you know, or china. Anything you feel you don't need —'

Miss Ledwitch regretted the impulse as soon as the gate had swung shut. She watched Mrs Mead patter down the lane, carrying a skirt made in 1923, a black silk shawl with moth-holes, a book on the construction of the Suez Canal, a set of Snakes and Ladders, and the blue vase. She was being torn in three directions; by relief at getting it out of the way, by the dreadful pang of parting with it, and by a still worse pang of conscience at handing over Miss Pennyfield or Miss Pennyfield's mother to yet another market. The last two emotions won, and only a firm hold on the oak beams of the porch and the thought of what people would say restrained Miss Ledwitch from rushing in pursuit of the vase and snatching it from its perch on Snakes and Ladders. She went indoors with a hangdog air.

Though she had meant to go to the jumble sale, she stayed at home instead. The last thing she wanted was to see who bought the vase. Sitting with her conscience was painful; at half-past three she put on her moleskin jacket, took a cherry-wood stick and started to walk the deserted lanes. Leaves choked the ditches and hung spinning on the ends of twigs. It was warm for November; in the shelter of the banks the warmth smelt like a compost heap. Miss Ledwitch walked briskly and tried to take her mind off by repeating *The Lady of Shalott*, a poem which she found sad but invariably soothing. Returning by a different route, remembering too late where she was, she had to pass Miss Pennyfield's house; guilt and remorse seized her, she dropped her eyes and began to

scurry by. A black saloon car stood outside the gate, and a man sat in the car, so quietly she did not notice him; her heart thudded when he let down the window. He called to her, 'Excuse me; is this Willowplace?'

Miss Ledwitch looked at him consideringly, past him to the dark and blank house in the meadows threaded with water, and back again. He seemed harmless, middle-aged, with thick glasses. She said, 'Yes. But it's empty; Miss Pennyfield —'

'I know,' said the man. 'She was my aunt, you see. I was on my way through – I thought I'd take a look at the place. I've never been here. Now that I've seen it I must say I'm not sorry I kept away.'

'The house is quite dry,' said Miss Ledwitch anxiously.

'Is it? I should have thought – I suppose you knew my aunt, in a place this size. I used to see a lot of her, ten or fifteen years ago – she lived in London then – but this and that happened, I've been abroad, and the war, you know . . . I'm told she turned eccentric, too.'

Miss Ledwitch stopped fidgeting and laid her hand on the lowered window. Her protuberant eyes fixed on him with unnerving intensity. She said, 'I – we wondered why the funeral was in London.'

'Oh – family gathering,' said Miss Pennyfield's nephew, moving one shoulder. 'Parents were buried there. I can't see that it matters, myself, can you?'

Buried! Miss Ledwitch swallowed and moved her lips. She leaned towards the window, hesitated, looked up and down the empty lane, and said at last, 'I wonder if you remember her blue vase? It had three cherubs on it. I always admired it so much.'

'Like an urn – of course I remember it. She used to keep her editors' regrets inside it. She —'

'I beg your pardon?'

'She wrote, you know – or perhaps you didn't. Pieces about wild animals; Brother Otter and so on; no doubt you know the line. Naturally no one wanted to publish them – not, however, from lack of trying on her part. She was a sticker, my aunt was. She burnt up all the refusal letters from editors and kept them in the vase and said they were the ashes of her literary hopes; a kind of joke, I always understood. A little whimsy – but of course she was. She had —'

Miss Ledwitch cut into his discourse with a peculiar sound. She looked at her watch; it was nearly half-past four. The jumble sale went on till five.

'Excuse me,' she said quickly. 'I've remembered I have a – I have to go. I'm so sorry. I do hope – Good afternoon . . .' Out of the corner of her eye she saw him turn his head and stare after her. Half-walking, half-running, she scuttled along the lane to the village, past her cottage, past the church, to the parish hall. She arrived crimson and panting. Though the stalls were two-thirds empty, a crowd still milled round them; but the vase was nowhere to be seen. Miss Ledwitch peered and bobbed and ducked and edged and pushed, all to no purpose. It was gone. Almost in tears, she made her way round to Mrs Mead. 'The blue vase I gave you,' she said, 'oh, do you remember who bought it?' 'Vase, dear?' said Mrs Mead. 'Oh, with the stars. No, I don't – Three-and-six, dear. Oh, is it? Well, two shillings. No, I'm afraid I've no idea; such a crowd we've had, and it was up the other end – Mrs Hacking

might, but she's gone. No, Mary, you'll rip it – put it down, there's a good girl. Four shillings, dear; yes, there's another somewhere. Miss Ledwitch, dear, you look so hot; have you been – oh, here it is, Alice. Say seven shillings the pair. All right, dear, six. . . .'

Sadly, Miss Ledwitch cast a despairing look round and wandered out.

Two days later she met Miss Howell, tramping up the lane from the direction of Willowplace. Miss Howell wore her hard-bitten tweeds, boots, and no hat, her short grey hair blew upright, she carried a gun under her arm and three rabbits swung from the other hand. Miss Ledwitch kept on the side away from the gun, and eyed the rabbits with distaste and suspicion, but with relief that they were not hares. 'Just coming to see you,' said Miss Howell. 'Cousin of mine arrives on Wednesday for a week. Beatrice, you know. She plays. Thought we might have a game, and ask poor Greene. How about Thursday?'

'That would be very nice,' said Miss Ledwitch, thinking how tactless.

'To remind us,' said Miss Howell, making matters worse. She leered at Miss Ledwitch and then at the rabbits. Miss Ledwitch stood and watched her out of sight, breathing quickly through her nose.

Miss Howell's thatched brick cottage was in its usual mess; guns and books lay around on Sheraton tables and smelly dogs on Hepplewhite chairs. Miss Ledwitch wore her grey, which showed hairs less than the black. Beatrice and Mrs Greene were waiting, Beatrice with an apprehensive air, for she was a cautious player and Miss Howell's bidding terrified her. Miss Ledwitch, however, took very little notice of either of them. Her how-do-you-do's died into a mutter; she was looking past them at Miss Howell's mantelpiece, on which, soaring divinely between a packet of Player's and a fishing reel, stood the blue vase.

'More reminders,' said Miss Howell, smirking. 'Goes well, don't you think? Picked it up at the jumble sale, for seven-and-six. I always liked it. She kept it full of ashes, God only knows what for.'

'What did you do with them?' said Miss Ledwitch in a dim voice.

'Do with what? Cut for partners —'

'The ashes.'

'You and Beatrice, and my deal. Ashes? Good God, what would anyone do with ashes? Threw 'em in the dustbin, of course. What would you have done?'

'I only wondered,' said Miss Ledwitch enviously. Her eyes turned back to the vase. It looked more beautiful than ever. To see it there was positive agony.

Miss Howell picked up her hand and said belligerently, 'What are you staring at me like that for, Ledwitch?'

'I was thinking how well you looked,' said Miss Ledwitch in despondent tones.

'Never felt better,' said Miss Howell. 'Three diamonds.'

Miss Ledwitch sighed, spread out her cards, leaned back to inspect them with her head tilted. 'Five spades,' she said irritably. Beatrice winced.

THE PROFESSOR'S
DAUGHTER

By the time she had walked past the Priory and up the steep hill from the town, Miss Jenner had made up her mind that father – she turned her eyes nostalgically upwards for a moment to the empty sky – would have agreed it was the right thing to do. Times change, my dear Evelina, times change; *tempora mutantur*: we must all live. She could almost hear his voice booming down. With an air of purpose, even of accepting a vocation, Miss Jenner set her hand in its clean grey cotton glove on the gate of the professor's house. Somewhere at the back of her head the thought still flickered and would not be quite extinguished – could it be possible that a Jenner should be reduced to this? But the cold breaths of circumstance and *tempora mutantur* blew on it. After all, said her pride, her resolution, it's not like manual labour. Miss Jenner opened the gate.

The professor's house, which was of dark-red brick and about a hundred and thirty years old, no more than just retained its dignity with an effort, like a clergyman's widow ripening into a weakness for port. Grass grew on the path, the open front door was painted in a faded blue; a child's tin wheelbarrow tipped drunkenly against the porch. Miss Jenner had expected a refined and tasteful order, and her resolve was a little shaken; but she remembered father's old friend, Professor Henwell, who in winter always wore an olive-green balaclava under a black soft hat, and achieving a patient smile at the eccentricities of genius she went on up the path and rang the bell.

Standing there in the porch, in her grey tweed suit and grey felt hat, Miss Jenner considered herself from without and was satisfied; no one could possibly mistake her for anything but what she was. Footsteps clipped on an uncarpeted floor. Here was the professor's wife, unexpectedly young, untidy, with tails of dark hair and a rash of pleasing freckles. She was conspicuously pregnant; the fact was underlined with a red belt, instead of being modestly hidden under a smock.

Miss Jenner swallowed a moment of frightful doubt. She thought a little wildly about demanding a subscription to the hospital, or the way to somewhere else, or even a glass of water; but '*Tempora mutantur*' she told herself, and inclining forward in a dignified manner she said, 'Good afternoon. You must be Mrs Greye.'

'Yes. Yes, I am,' said the professor's wife, looking apprehensive.

'My name is Jenner. I believe the professor was at one time acquainted with my late father, the Reverend Ignatius Jenner.'

'Oh yes,' said the professor's wife. 'Do come in.' Blast, she said to herself briefly. Blast.

Miss Jenner took in the living-room with a glance like the sweep of a scythe. Too full of books, too empty of furniture; wild flowers in a glass jar, smudges of dust on a floor nearly bare of rugs. Her plans for a social chat, for a discreet leading-up to the distasteful point of her visit, melted away. She wanted to get it over. She sat down on the edge of a green armchair, and said, 'I must explain why I am here. I saw your advertisement in the window of The Spinning Wheel, for someone to take your little girl out in the afternoons. Now that Father has passed on' – Miss Jenner's upward glance was a thought perfunctory, she was occupied with the difficult present – 'I have come down here and taken furnished rooms. I have so much spare time that I feel I should like to do something to help those less fortunately placed. If you think I should be suitable, perhaps you would let me take your little one off your hands for the hours you suggest – weather permitting, of course. I'm afraid I have a silly tendency to bronchitis, but any other time when it's fine . . .' Miss Jenner repressed a disinclination to stop talking; unable to make up her mind whether she was doing well or not, she looked anxiously at her umbrella.

'Oh yes, well – it's very kind of you,' said the professor's wife, quite taken by surprise. 'I really do want —' Thoughts elbowed one another into her head. Eminently conscientious. A sticky business about offering the money – perhaps a sealed envelope, yes, I suppose that would be genteel. Somehow I can't see Britta with her; no, she's really so very . . .

'I love children,' said Miss Jenner rather suddenly. She had just realised that this was what should have come first.

'Well – I'd be awfully grateful,' said the professor's wife, mentally shutting her eyes, taking the plunge. 'But I mean,' she said, 'the only thing is, I hope you won't find Britta too exhausting. I haven't any help in the house, you see, and what with this baby' – Miss Jenner, shocked, avoided the gesture and turned her eyes to the window – 'I just can't manage to get out twice in the day. She ought to go out in the afternoons. Fresh air —'

'Nothing like it,' said Miss Jenner reverently.

'The thing is, she's not four yet but she's horribly precocious. I mean, she has a fearful imagination. I don't think I spoil her, but it does make things difficult.'

'Oh, you mustn't let that worry you. I remember when I was quite a tiny thing, no bigger than Britta – is it? Did I quite catch her name? How quaint; is it short for Britannia?'

'No,' said the professor's wife rather loudly, 'it's a Danish name. I am half Danish.'

'Oh. I was saying, I remembered being quite convinced that a little fairy lived in each of the flowers in the garden. Sometimes I think I really *did* see them. Oh, all children are alike, you know – they all have these charming fancies.'

'Yes,' the professor's wife said doubtfully. 'Oh yes, I suppose so.'

'Then it's all settled,' cried Miss Jenner with temperate relief. But an awful thought struck her: would Mrs Greye be afraid to offer her money? Miss Jenner almost paled. She was suffering this humiliation solely for the sake of thirty shillings extra a week, solely, that is, for what they signified

– for the small things that made all the difference – the library subscription, the tomato ketchup, the morning coffee and the shillings to feed the meter. But the professor's wife, looking embarrassed, saved her by saying, 'I'm afraid I can't afford more than one pound ten, if that's all right.'

'Oh, perfectly all right; yes, indeed,' said Miss Jenner quite gaily, even forgetting in her relief to be ashamed. Now that everything was straightened out she found it possible to relax; now for the first time her conscious attention was drawn to a chain of little rustling and fidgeting noises from somewhere down beside her chair. Miss Jenner dropped a casual glance and found it resting (turning in a flash from casual to horrified) on an open green canvas Gladstone bag in which, on a bed of shredded newspaper, a striped cat was in the act of producing its third kitten. If she had seen a coil of ectoplasm or a decapitated head Miss Jenner could not have leapt more precipitately from her chair.

'I'm sorry, did Alice startle you?' said the professor's wife, getting up and bending with difficulty over the Gladstone bag. 'I have to have her in here – she gets in a state if I'm not around. Three. Probably two more to come, yes, it feels at least two. I say, the black one's lovely – look, it hasn't any white at all. The father has white feet. I like them all black, don't you?'

'I think I should be going,' said Miss Jenner. 'I mustn't keep you.'

The professor's wife straightened up. 'I'm sorry you can't see Britta today. She's gone to tea with the Hays' children.'

'I think that was very wise of you,' said Miss Jenner.

Puzzled, the professor's wife looked at her vaguely. Then the light broke. 'Oh yes,' she said in a shaking voice. She put her hand up to her face, and led the way to the door.

Shortly after two the next afternoon Miss Jenner walked down the hill from the professor's house. She clutched Britta kindly but desperately by the hand. The weather had failed her. It wasn't raining, the bright sun flashed in an eggshell sky, and here she was, a worker, a Domestic Help, shepherding a stranger's offspring. It walked beside her quite willingly, with an abstracted composure, in silence. Miss Jenner in fact was favourably surprised by Britta; she seemed a model child. Quiet but not shy. Clean and neat. Healthy, even pretty. Miss Jenner looked down at the china skin touched with rose, the large light blue-grey eyes, the dark hair which did not curl but grew in upward arcs from the temples and round the head. She was dressed austerely in a small tailored navy coat with a velvet collar, long grey socks and minute black shoes. She wore no hat. Miss Jenner liked to see little girls in white or pink, in muslin and a frill or two, but she had to admit that Britta looked tidy and well-bred, and that was considerably more than she had expected. Sighing, she plunged into her duty. 'Well, Britta; do you like this lovely sunshine?'

'I'm aren't Britta,' said the professor's daughter. 'I'm a bull.'

'Oh no,' said Miss Jenner, appalled, after a pause. 'That's not nice at all. You're a little girl.'

'I'm a *bull*,' said Britta on a rising note. She stopped walking and let go of Miss Jenner's hand. Out of the corner

of her eye Miss Jenner saw the Vicar's approach from farther down the hill. She bit the finger of her grey glove. 'I know what,' she said. 'We'll go down to the gardens where the flowers are and see if we can see a fairy, shall we?'

'Which flowers?' said Britta, accepting the change of subject and taking Miss Jenner's hand again.

'The little red ones on the tree.'

'The japonica?'

Miss Jenner flinched; surely children of not yet four lisped in words of one syllable. To her prodigious relief the Vicar disappeared through the gate of a house. She led Britta past it and down to the bottom of the hill, into the public gardens, across to the japonica trained against the stone wall. 'Now,' she said, 'now we must watch very carefully.' Britta fixed her large light eyes with gratifying interest on the flowers. 'There!' cried Miss Jenner, encouraged. 'There! In that one, did you see it? A little red fairy.'

'In this one?'

'Yes. With little green wings.'

'It's still there.'

'So it is,' said Miss Jenner, beginning to feel quite competent. 'So it is. Isn't it lovely?'

Britta stretched up her hand in a knitted glove and picked something invisible between finger and thumb. She bent down and put it on the stone paving. With amiable concentration she stamped on it three times.

'I've killed it,' she said.

Miss Jenner opened her mouth and shut it again. At last she said, 'Let's go over to the bandstand.' In silence they walked down the path to the ring of painted iron seats, the painted tin roof fluted like a shell, with the hills behind. After taking off her glove and testing one of the seats with the back of her hand to see if it was damp Miss Jenner allowed herself to sit down; she felt she needed a short pause. After the pause conscience and the thirty shillings a week began to nag at her.

'Britta,' she said, 'what did you do this morning? Did you play with your dollies?'

'I did an operation on my bear.'

Miss Jenner looked imploringly at the bandstand.

'I putted him on a silver trolley,' said Britta. 'I gave him a prick in his arm and then I wheeled him into the theatre, and then I shaved his chest with my little razor and then I putted a thing over his face, and I said "If you don't like the smell blow it away", and then he went to sleep; and then I cutted his liver out because it was bad, and I gived it to Alice, and then I wiped my little knife and I sewed him up with a needle and I put him back to bed with a receiver 'case he sicked.'

'You're not a nice little girl to play games like that,' said Miss Jenner after a long silence.

'I'm aren't a little girl. I'm a bull.'

'Britta, you're not a bull. Don't say that again.'

'I'm *are*,' said Britta violently, going pink.

'We'll go and walk down to the shops,' said Miss Jenner, equally but less becomingly pink. She looked at her watch; it said half-past two. She listened to it; it ticked complacently. They went down a flight of steps to the iron gates and out into the street. Britta refused Miss Jenner's silently offered hand. She walked holding her arms out obliquely at the level of her

chest, with an air of pride, apparently grasping something unseen.

'Hold my hand, Britta,' said Miss Jenner.

'I can't hold your hand,' said Britta. 'I'm wheeling my bicycle.'

'You're not wheeling a bicycle. Hold my hand and don't be ridiculous.'

'I'm ARE. This is my bicycle and I'm wheeling it along the gutter.' Britta ignored Miss Jenner. Fifty yards farther on she stopped and passionately shook the invisible handlebars; she emitted a contralto roar.

'*Britta!*' said Miss Jenner.

'The pedal's sticked. My pedal's sticked and it won't go. *You* make my pedal go,' said Britta in a mounting tune of fury.

With a violent effort Miss Jenner swallowed a note of the same pitch. She said, 'Everyone is looking at us. Come along *at once!*'

Britta squatted on the pavement – one raised hand supported the handlebars and with the other she made frenzied hammering gestures. Agonised, Miss Jenner stood as far away as she dared, suffering (as St Sebastian suffered the arrows) the amused stares of passers-by. Britta got up. 'It goes now,' she said, and went on wheeling.

Miss Chiffley was on them before Miss Jenner saw her approach. Now there was no time to dive across the road, not a hope of scuttling into the nearest shop. 'My *dear* Miss Jenner,' said Miss Chiffley, 'just whom I was hoping to see. I'm going to carry you off to Smith's to help me choose some books. Now, I won't take no for an answer.'

Miss Jenner swallowed again. Out of the corner of her eye she saw the bicycle being propped against the kerb. It appeared to fall down; Britta muttered something, picked it up, made circular movements with one leg. Miss Jenner wondered frantically if she could disown Britta altogether and get away with some excuse.

But it was no good; it wasn't going to work. The bicycle was safely propped and Britta edged up to Miss Chiffley, staring. Miss Chiffley was indeed imposing: in her burgundy tweeds she swelled outwards, towered upwards towards the sky.

'You've got a little tiny kitty on your back,' said Britta, enthralled. 'Look – it's crawling up on your shoulder. A little tiny green kitty. There it goes!'

Miss Chiffley bent majestically but with a touch of uneasiness. 'A what, dear?'

'I'm aren't a dear,' said Britta. 'I'm a bull.'

Miss Jenner hurried into the breach. 'This is Professor Greye's little girl. He is, that is to say he was, a great friend of my dear father's, and I am taking her out for the afternoon, just for today – at the moment her mother isn't able —'

'My mummy,' said Britta with casual interest, 'my mummy's got a baby inside —'

'Britta!' cried Miss Jenner, finding her presence of mind in extreme crisis, 'Britta, look at the lovely white horse!'

'I'm aren't Britta. I said, I'm a BULL.'

'A difficult child,' said Miss Chiffley severely.

Miss Jenner felt the chill of disapproval. She deeply admired Miss Chiffley, who was rich and of good family; she was goaded into authority. 'Don't be ridiculous, Britta,'

she said. 'You're a very naughty little girl. Don't say that
again.'

Britta turned her head away from Miss Jenner. Her gaze
fell on the kerb. She gave a howl. 'My bicycle's falled over! It's
falled over, look!'

'You haven't got a bicycle,' said Miss Jenner, losing control.
'Be quiet *this minute!*'

'I have got a bicycle! I have! It's falled over. You pick it up;
you pick my bicycle up for me!'

'I shall take you home this minute and tell your mother.'
Beneath her panic Miss Jenner had a muddled and unhappy
feeling that she was falling into every possible error open to
the caretaker of a child. 'Miss Chiffley, really I don't know how
to apologise.'

'My dear Miss Jenner,' said Miss Chiffley, 'it's certainly not
your fault. Does her mother . . . is she . . .?'

They mumbled together, turning their heads towards
the hills, dropping oblique glances at Britta. Miss Jenner
was a little relieved to see that Britta stood in momentary
silence; but the next glance showed only too clearly what
was on her mind. The penetrating stare was fixed on Miss
Chiffley's monumental bosom. Miss Jenner was past being
capable of red-herring tactics. She could only advance her
departure.

Britta's eyes, large, blank and brilliant, the colour of a
sunless sea, went up to Miss Chiffley's face and down again.
She took no notice at all of Miss Jenner.

'You've got a baby in there,' said Britta. 'You've got a baby
like my mummy. Haven't you?'

Miss Jenner threw in her hand. Without a word to Miss Chiffley she seized Britta by the elbow and hauled her up the street.

Looking cleaner, tidier and already more composed, the professor's wife poured richly chestnut-coloured tea into two thick white cups. Miss Jenner sat on the edge of the armchair. 'Surely it encourages untruthfulness,' she was saying.

'I don't look at it from the moral standard,' said the professor's wife. 'If they want to see things I don't see why they should be thwarted. It's much less tiring for everybody if we see them too.'

'It seems to me highly immoral,' said Miss Jenner.

'You said you used to see fairies.'

Miss Jenner said, 'That, I think, is different.'

Britta came in, still wearing her coat. She said, 'I've put my bicycle away in the shed.'

'I hope not pushed against my mangle.'

'No,' said Britta, 'in the corner all by its selluf.'

'Take your coat off and hang it up, and put your slippers on and come and have your tea.' The professor's wife looked at Miss Jenner. Miss Jenner sat stiffly upright; her mouth was drawn together and her nose red. The professor's wife sighed.

'She said I hadn't got a bicycle,' said Britta an hour later, buttoning up her pyjamas.

'Well, never mind. We know you have.'

'She won't come any more, will she?' said Britta. 'I don't want her to come any more.'

'No,' said the professor's wife, 'no, she won't come any more.'

'There's a little tiny red hedgehog on that curtain, look.'

The professor's wife picked it off, the unseen hedgehog, and held it in her hands. 'I'll take it downstairs,' she said. She turned out the light and shut the door; and because she was thinking of Miss Jenner she carried it in her hands with absent care all the way down to the kitchen.

ROLLIVER

The second train left them on a clear platform and dwindled away, half an hour late, panting, into the pellucid distance. Celia sat down on her suitcase, next to some milk churns and a large wire and wicker box full of carrier pigeons. She saw that Henry was already exasperated by the journey; though he had slept soundly in the night express from London he insisted he hadn't. At the main line junction where they had breakfasted on coffee and sandwiches at the station buffet he kept saying, 'I didn't go off for a second.' The bread was stale, he said, the coffee not fit to drink; the second train came in twenty minutes late and he leaned back in a corner seat as if the express had been the Trans-Siberian. Now he fussed among the churns and the pigeons, worrying about missing the connection.

'Don't, Henry,' said Celia, sitting there wrapped in peace. 'Don't shunt around. It's perfectly all right; however late it is they wait for it.'

Henry stopped fretting and looked guilty. After all the planning and the anticipation he felt himself behaving like a heel; he came over and touched her shoulder. Something almost calculating in her eye impelled him to say 'Forgive me.'

Celia smiled but made no answer. She was thinking that in spite of his unshaven chin and the batterings and rumplings of the journey Henry had too worldly an air for this station; his tweeds faintly suggested the stage. For the first time since they had met she saw him out of his natural (but could one call Henry's background natural?) – his normal setting, the axis round which revolved waiters, secretaries, taxi-drivers, board-meetings and junior typists; she saw in his expression not only the frustration of rural travel but the conviction that in four days without its managing director the firm would dissolve in ruin. She thought, If I marry Henry I marry Stendwell Limited and I should turn into a preference share.

'What are you smiling at?' said Henry. 'Why doesn't the blasted train come in? Celia, are you sure it hasn't gone?'

'It never did,' she said tranquilly. 'It was always late. And why should it go, Henry? It doesn't have to come back till half past ten. And you're looking in the wrong direction; it comes from up that way because it spends the night in a little shed round the bend somewhere. I always wanted to see where Rolliver lived, but I never did manage it.'

'Now how can you possibly know what goes on after twenty years, and who in hell's name is Rolliver?'

'Do things look as if they've changed in twenty years here?' said Celia. 'Rolliver is the train. Everyone called it that and nobody knew why.'

Henry frowned, sucked down his upper lip, took out his gold cigarette-case and looked fretfully at its contents. Around

them the station and the countryside were deserted; after the summer storms in the night the air was as clear and bright as glass. It was a quarter past nine. Sunlight poured flashing out of the sky on the wooded hills, the platform, the steel rails beautifully curving out of sight. In their wicker box the pigeons scratched and murmured, rustling their dry wings. Henry waltzed off to look for someone he could legitimately badger, and Celia, left sitting placidly, forgot him at once. Nothing had changed; even the roses along the platform fence were still red, watercress and forget-me-nots still grew in the stream below it. She saw herself a child of ten, the year they had left for Hampshire, climbing through the trellis to pull watercress out of the ditch. Here she sat and twenty years had altered her, but the ditch was still the same. Twenty years had left her hair mouse-coloured but curled it short, had reddened her mouth, had left her eyes slate-blue but changed the kind and compass of their vision, had replaced navy reefer coats and black lace-ups by the costly suit of slate-blue linen, the soft red leather shoes; twenty years had given her the flat in Cheyne Walk, the office in Hanover Square; and now the little bouquet, the bonus, a weekend with a managing director met but a month ago. Celia drifted back to the present; am I, am I in love with Henry?

He had disappeared. Celia looked up the platform in time to see emerge, from the door through which he had vanished, a white goat. For a lunatic moment she asked herself if it was Henry, transformed by some rustic magic; the notion pleased her, and she lifted her face and smiled. The goat was tied apparently to the door-handle; it made an affable pass at

Henry as he edged through and hastened out of range towards Celia and the churns and pigeons. He shook back his sleeve to reveal his watch, frowned at it, said disbelievingly, 'He seems to think it's coming.' And sure enough, beyond his shoulder, Celia saw it loitering askew and backwards round the bend. Twenty years had left Rolliver unchanged, but the progress of main-line rolling stock had endowed it in contrast with a rich period flavour; it now edged on the eccentric. In this distorting mirror it reflected Celia's memory: had the one carriage always been quite so high, the funnel quite so tall? Were other trains on curving lines quite so inevitably one side or the other of perpendicular? Henry's head was turned over his shoulder to its approach. His profile was aghast. 'Good God,' he said, when it rocked to a standstill with the single door six feet from his nose. 'Is it safe? Where's the first class?'

'There isn't a first class,' said Celia. Henry seemed mildly tolerant, was perhaps for the moment disarmed. 'What do you expect? Only ordinary trains have such refinements.'

Henry was skirmishing with the door. 'It's locked. It would be.'

Celia opened it inwards. Without indecision she turned into the compartment on the left, into the seat on the platform side next to the window that opened; she had sat down before she realised this had always been her place. Still nothing had changed or even faded; the wiry dark-red upholstery, the iron-framed seats, the aisle of brown linoleum down the middle, the brownish photographs of a castle, a shore, a river, might have been embalmed in time. 'Henry

– oh, Henry, look.' She touched the letters badly cut on the window frame. 'CSL I did that the day we left for good. I do remember it so well; it was raining and I had the cat on my lap in a box. And now they're still here.'

'Celia,' said Henry, 'if it's the same train it's hardly surprising. You don't have to go off in an emotional frenzy.' She looked at him to see if he was smiling; he was not. She let down the window and leaned out over the platform. After a moment he sniffed – or perhaps it was a sigh – and lowered the adjoining one. Six yards away the goat was being coaxed, bullied, and finally lifted bodily into the luggage van by the engine-driver and the fireman (who were not the same ones as twenty years ago) and the station official (who was in shirt-sleeves and whose status was therefore a little difficult to place). After the goat went the pigeons. There seemed to be no other passengers. The driver hitched up his overalls and began to potter in the direction of the engine, trying in passing the handle of the door and nodding to Celia and Henry. Celia's face appeared to encourage him. He said, 'Here's Sam Lisboyne's goat over to Fordenbarton.'

'I'm glad you got her in all right.'

'Yu ready to be off?' asked the driver.

'I think so, thank you,' said Celia. Henry opened his mouth and shut it again. The driver climbed in, and Rolliver made a noise like a soda-water siphon and eased off from the platform.

'Dear Henry,' said Celia, 'never mind. We're bound to get there soon.' Henry's expression was incredulous; he was watching the station official in shirt-sleeves lower the signal

from a large naked lever by the rose-grown fence, a second after they passed it. He raised it again immediately; it was a little ritual he seemed to enjoy; taking off his cap, throwing his cigarette in the stream, he picked a rose and slid out of Henry's sight. Celia felt that Henry was composing a letter to the railway company. Dear Sirs, said his flaring nostrils, his outraged eye, It is my duty in the interests of public safety to bring to your notice . . . She said to herself, Oh dear; oh hell, she said; he was so nice in London. Nice? Well, perhaps interesting; intelligent; efficient; pleasant to go out with, to be managed by for a change, to have as an organiser of one's entertainment. But nice . . . Well. She looked consideringly at Henry's face, at his pleasing and urbane yet hawk-like features now iced with severity.

'One door,' said Henry with cold disapproval, long past saying the right thing or even knowing the right thing to say, 'One door for the whole train, and it holds –' his eye flickered in the rhythm of calculation, '– it holds quite fifty people. And of all things opening *inwards*. Outrageous. If there were a fire —'

'Two doors,' said Celia. 'One each side.'

'– Or any other accident,' said Henry, taking no notice, 'the whole place would be a death-trap. Literally a death-trap. I am —'

'That it *can* hold fifty people,' said Celia, 'isn't to say it ever has. On market days there used to be fifteen or so. And I suppose one could get out of the windows. Anyway, nothing ever has happened; why should it?'

'I don't like the way it leans.'

Celia turned her head away with faint exasperation. In contrast to the upright scenery Henry did indeed look a little like someone shot obliquely in a highbrow film. Rolliver was negotiating one of the curves, and by leaning her temple against the window she could see the single track snaking ahead between the river and an overgrown cutting in the hillside. The half-forgotten entrancing view reminded her that already she had missed some of it listening to Henry blathering about fires and death-traps. Nothing would make her say another word. Henry sat haggardly, frowning and pressing his lips together when Rolliver bounded lurching at a fresh curve and settled on the other side of the vertical. Henry must not be allowed to spoil the journey. But it was too late; Celia was cold with the remembered childish sense of irritation towards the people who sniff at one's passions, engendering at once a savage possessiveness and the guilt of doubt and disloyalty. Here was Henry, a mockery of Henry in London, an urban greenhouse plant that withered in the country air. But Henry had not reached his city stature for nothing; no, he knew what she was thinking. He considered his next move, he gave it serious thought, he leaned towards her and said again, 'Forgive me, Celia. I'm sorry. I'm an impatient traveller and not used to incompetence, and it's been a long journey. All I want is to arrive.'

Celia was easily touched by apologies, but this one, too discreetly rehearsed in silence, left her cold. It was as though Henry, perhaps unwillingly, had handed her in the last sentence the desire governing not his present circumstances but his life. All he wants is to arrive.

'Look at the river,' she said. 'It's beautiful, isn't it? We used to glue our noses to the glass and watch for herons.'

'Charming,' said Henry, flicking towards the river the kind of glance he would have awarded a gasometer. 'How long did you say this trip takes?'

'I can't just remember exactly. It's thirteen miles, I think, and there are two stations in between. Truly, Henry, it won't be long now.'

'Ah well,' Henry said in resignation, 'a hot bath and a damned good lunch and I'll be a new man. I think I'd better ring the office this afternoon.'

As clearly as if the scene were being acted near her nose on the window's stage instead of fished from recollections twenty years old, Celia saw at once the horrid repercussions of Henry's arrival; Rolliver was still the same; why should time have changed The Compasses? Once they had stayed there for three days, while the house was being painted. The bath water had been tepid; on and off a gush of black feathers had irrationally burst from the tap. Boiled beef for two days and boiled mutton on the third were engraved on her memory by the sharp edge of her mother's contempt; her father's oaths on the telephone when he tried to ring up the builder at Fordenbarton she could have repeated word for word. No cobbled yards, no timbers and rose-red bricks would reconcile Henry to black feathers and boiled beef and the battle for Trunks. She looked at him, and sighed, and turned again to the window; polished with dappled light the river curled past between the woods, and at once, in the shallow water near the bank, she saw a heron standing, the lovely fantastic bird

like no other bird on earth to her. 'Oh, look!' she cried, a childhood reflex, Henry becoming Andrew her brother. She regretted calling Henry's attention to it. Henry would say 'What is it?' He did.

Rolliver achieved the first station, leaning a little towards the yellow roses across the platform. Defensively Celia hoped for another passenger, to justify the train's existence. Providence rewarded her with malice; she could not help laughing at Henry's unbelieving stare. She had never seen a cat more baroquely decorated in white, black and red-gold. It swayed into the carriage, looked through rather than at Henry, and jumped into the corner seat near the door. Henry sucked down his lip and eloquently said nothing. Celia leaned out of the window. An old man was propped among the roses. She called to him, 'There's a cat here.'

'Ar,' he said.

'Shall I put it on the platform? The train's going, I think.'

''E don't du no 'arm. 'Tes the same every day – 'e've a fancy for goen to St Thomas and 'e'm back come dinnertime. Us lets un go.'

'Oh,' said Celia. She smiled at the old man. The train started. Henry leaned back against what should have been the padded seat; it was not. He gave an anguished frown, slid down till the naked iron caught him across the base of his skull, shut his eyes and said 'T-t-t.' Celia looked from the river to the cat, admiring its monumental calm, from the cat back to the river, watching for herons. Between the hillside and the bank the serpentine track tilted Rolliver to the one side, to the other, to the one and back again. With this gentle

rocking motion they would pass the calm reaches like dark glass pools where the trees bent to touch their reflected leaves, and past the stretches of water crinkling and curling over stones, around smooth rocks. Henry tried to resist the insidious leaning and swaying. Rolliver won. Uneasy, hungry, dirty and cross, Henry nevertheless went to sleep.

He woke with a start; his queasy consciousness swam up into silence. They were no longer moving and through the window he saw only the gliding river and the trees and the sun. Though he was ready to believe almost anything of Rolliver, there was not a vestige of a station in sight. He turned to Celia to say '*Now* what the —'; but Celia, even Celia, was gone too. In its corner the baroque cat sat with half-shut eyes. Henry said something voiceless to himself and leaned out of the window. Twenty yards in front of the engine he saw a tree lying across the track. Five men stood round it; two of them were gently stroking it with a cross-cut saw, and the other three were talking to Celia. She leaned against a branch and on a twig beside her hung her slate-blue linen jacket; her arms were bare, in one hand she held a bunch of moon-daisies and in the other a cigarette. It was so quiet that when the men with the saw stopped for a rest – about every twelfth stroke – Henry heard through his rising fury not only their voices and the faint hiss from the engine but the pigeons rustling and roucouling in the luggage van and a thudding sound that must be the goat. Nothing would make him call to Celia; she would not turn her head and see him; fuming, invoking Heaven to strike with sudden lightning all railways and Rolliver in particular, he stayed with his head stuck out of the window in the sunlight smelling of hay and wet stones.

After some time the tree fell into two pieces. The men with the saw looked at it with mild surprise; they got together with the others, achieved at last some degree of organisation, and lifted it off the track. There were the branches and twigs to be picked up, the words to be bandied with the engine-driver and the fireman, whom Henry now saw sitting on the farther bank sharing something out of a paper bag. Celia brushed pieces of stick off the rails, with her red gloves held in one hand. The way she talked to the men, and stood up to shade her eyes and stare at the river, drove Henry away from the window to lean back in anger and frustration against the unrelenting seat. Seven more minutes passed before she came into the carriage. Henry eased his watch from his sleeve. It said ten-fifteen.

Rolliver made a Henryish sound and eased off past a mountain of branches and twigs. Celia sat down opposite him, smiling, with her cheeks pink; he saw for the first time a freckle or two on her nose, she carried her jacket on her bare arm, and he thought in his annoyance, She looks bucolic, disapprovingly, for he liked city women, smooth and powdered pale. 'You woke up,' she said. 'Oh, did you see the tree?'

'I did,' said Henry acidly. 'Doubtless typical. We might have run into it; and of course it occurred to no one to telephone the station.'

'Oddly enough,' said Celia, surprising herself, 'it just happens there isn't a callbox on this stretch of the river.' Henry seemed taken aback; easy sarcasm was not one of her habits.

She added more calmly, 'It was blown down in the night and no one found it till an hour ago. They did send someone round the bend to stop the train. You were asleep.'

Henry made no answer; he gave her a sidelong and curious glance, spread one groomed hand on his knee and watched it attentively, as if he expected it to perform some acrobatic trick of its own accord. Celia offered him, if he cared to look at it, a gently forbidding profile, an eye intently roving the sliding water for the sight of a heron. When she saw one it was lifting from the shallows on its vast and slow wings, trailing its legs like straws behind it; she followed its flight across the sky in silence. She was thinking how magical this journey could have been, with Rolliver and the river, the cat, the goats and pigeons and the tree; how magical, but for Henry.

They reached the station at Fordenbarton. Henry was sunk in a kind of expectant gloom; no one, however, got on, and nothing was disembarked. The station official, this time a female, passed the time of day with the driver, and when they were about to tear themselves away Celia remembered the goat. She put her head out of the window and said, 'There's a goat for Mr Lisboyne in the van.'

'T-t,' said Henry under his breath. The goat did not want to alight; it took the united efforts of the woman, the engine-driver and the fireman to get it down to the platform. Tied to the fence, it chewed paper; its slotted pupils fixed on Celia a resentful stare. The woman nodded at her and smiled. In a leisurely manner she and the driver and the fireman drifted talking up the platform and repeated the parting scene.

Rolliver steamed off, only to be recalled twenty yards further on by an ear-splitting howl. Celia looked out again. Gesturing frenziedly, the woman screamed at the engine-driver. Out of the corner of her eye Celia saw Henry's face; she blushed for Rolliver. They backed in again. The woman opened the door, and in its furious dignity the cat was re-embarked. Celia could no longer think of anything to say. It seemed to her that Rolliver had achieved the ultimate touch of malice; twenty years of rehearsal could hardly have produced a journey more nicely calculated to ruin her relationship with Henry. Defensive pique and a dread of being snubbed or setting light to his plainly smouldering exasperation prevented her from talking lightly of something else, a civilised course which in London, if a like situation had arisen, she would not have thought twice about. But some kind of repentant effort was perhaps stirring in Henry; he looked up at the roof, and, in a tone that Celia tried to interpret as reconciling, said, 'How do they light it? Or doesn't it go at night?'

Celia wished he would get off the subject altogether; into a debate on agriculture or Persian carpets she could have flung herself amiably and with relief. 'Oh yes,' she said, 'in the winter it does. It's lit by gas.' It sounded, if Henry could be persuaded to leave it at that, rustic but quite efficient. She remembered standing on the home platform, at tea-time one winter's day, to see the train leave; with pink noses and cold hands, she and Andrew put off the pleasure of buttered toast already waiting, to watch the ritual of the lamps, to watch the engine-driver (then a square man with a moustache) thrust an oil-can into the engine's red-hot belly and carry it, gushing

flame, to light first the yellow lantern at the front and then the red one at the back; after that he would climb into the train and open, one after the other, the glass covers along the roof. Celia could see it now, as clearly as she saw the lamps unchanged above her head after twenty years; the faces of the people in the darkening carriage upturned and intent in the leaping flame, and the greenish still light spreading over them, and Rolliver going off at last with the illumined windows, the red lantern, round the curve and out of sight in the dark. 'Gas,' said Henry. 'Good heavens.' He had made his social contribution; he lowered his head and relapsed into traveller's gloom, haunted by gross shapes, Outdatedness, Incompetence, Carelessness and Delay. Celia could almost see them hovering behind the seat.

Ford St Thomas and the end of the journey approached. Leaning her cheek against the warm glass, Celia saw the village crowning the hill, half a mile behind the station, half a mile for which Henry would certainly want a taxi. She saw, no bigger in the distance than a child's bricks, the square white house where she had been born and the church tower with a Tudor gable on top. 'Here we are,' she said to Henry. This platform too was almost deserted; only the station-master, a woman and a child watched them arrive. The small boy held the woman's hand and bounced up and down. 'Rolliver! Rolliver!' he shouted. The cat uncoiled itself and stretched. Celia climbed down into the sunlight, and behind her, moving stiffly as if he had just crossed Europe, came Henry with the suitcases. He put them down and dug irritably in his sleeve for his watch. 'Ten thirty-five. It's late already, going back.'

'It will go straight off,' said Celia. 'Anyway, we're here; it doesn't matter what it does now.'

'For all I care,' said Henry, fumbling in his pockets and turning a venomous glare on Rolliver, 'it can now disintegrate. A good thing if it did. Where did I put those blasted tickets?'

Celia looked at him and shut her mouth over the reply on her tongue. Trained in the urban law, Henry searched furiously, though there was no one to collect the tickets if he found them. A boy came through the gate and carried the wicker box of pigeons up the platform; there beside the flower-bed, the fence wreathed with honeysuckle, he opened the lid and let them go. He and Celia, the station-master, the driver and fireman, the woman and the child watched them rush and circle round the sky; only Henry, suffused with rage at his own incompetence, went on hunting and muttering. At last he found the tickets in a pocket of his notecase. The station-master took them indifferently, as if they were sandwich wrappings handed to him for salvage. The pigeons made up their common mind and flew off to the south-west; down the platform from the flower-bed strolled the cat, waving its tail.

'Now,' said Henry, 'where do I get a car?'

Celia saw further storms ahead. It was clearly no use suggesting that they walked. She said unwillingly, 'There's a sort of garage outside, across the road.'

'You stay here, with the suitcases. If the car is anything like the train —' Henry left this menacing sentence unfinished and strode off into the outer world. With a despairing and apprehensive air Celia watched him go; she knew only too

well what Henry would be faced with at the garage, and had now a clearish idea of what the garage would be up against in Henry. She sat down, sighing, and considered the next few days. She thought about the bath water, the feathers, the boiled mutton, the telephone, the village natives, the single shop, the cowsheds next to The Compasses, the bats, the owls, the return journey in Rolliver. Shocked at herself but stubbornly admitting the emotion, she passionately wished she had come back in no one's company but her own. Or at least, she said to herself with agonising candour, at least in anyone's but Henry's. Henry is going to shatter my early life within an hour.

Rolliver stopped hissing, and when she turned her head she saw the driver climbing into the engine. Out of the end window the cat, alone in the carriage, thrust a white and red-gold head with two black ears. At the thought of that lovely impending journey with no one but the cat to see it Celia lost her head entirely. She picked up her suitcase and climbed on a lunatic impulse back through the inward-opening door, at the very moment when Rolliver lurched, puffed and departed. The station-master's open mouth slid past her. 'I'll pay the other end,' she called to it. Rolliver leaned over to the left and eased out of sight round the bend.

On the platform lay Henry's suitcase, naked and alone. The station-master, coming at last out of a trance over the whole odd situation, picked it up and bore it into the office. He put it on a bench in the corner, away from the crate, the pram and the things tied up in sacking that were littered around, rummaged in the desk for a piece of tattered

cardboard, propped it on top, and went off to make some tea. The piece of cardboard had black shiny letters erratically stuck on it. It confronted Henry when he came rampaging back looking for his suitcase and his Celia. It had slipped down sideways so that only part of it showed. It said:

LEFT

Persephone Books publishes forgotten fiction and non-fiction by unjustly neglected authors. The following titles are available: